Jo heard a familiar drawl

Abruptly, she stopped. For a moment she couldn't see him, then a gap opened around the bar and Dan came into view, talking to the manager, Anton.

Anton gesticulated to make a point and a beer bottle toppled off the counter. Dan caught it and looked up. Even in the dimly lit bar, his eyes were a piercing blue. Of course he'd known she was there. He smiled at her with all the old lazy affection, a smile as warm as a fire on a cold night, drawing her closer.

"Here comes my bride."

"Great joke." She stepped into her best mate's hug. "Really hilarious."

Dan's eyes gleamed. "Miss me?"

"No." She broke free only to be pulled into Anton's embrace.

"Congratulations, Jo. Sheesh, you're a dark horse. Why the hell didn't you tell your old gang?"

"Because this so-called wedding is just a joke."

Dan pulled a beer mat out of his jeans pocket and handed it to Anton. "Not so. I have a contract."

Dear Reader,

If you could compare writing books to scaling mountains this one would be Everest or Frodo and Sam's Mount Doom. Maybe because of the level of research, maybe because this is the first of a series and I had three other books in my head as I wrote it. Probably because I loved my characters so much and wanted to do them justice.

The initial idea—what if your best friend called in a joke wedding contract?—became a book about persevering against the odds. And boy, did I give my characters odds. But as true heroes do, they pushed through the challenges and eventually got to The End happily.

I hope you relish their journey as much as I did.

Karina Bliss

P.S. I love to hear from readers (see dedication!). You can email me at karina@karinabliss.com and visit my website, www.karinabliss.com.

Here Comes the Groom
Karina Bliss

HARLEQUIN®

TORONTO • NEW YORK • LONDON
AMSTERDAM • PARIS • SYDNEY • HAMBURG
STOCKHOLM • ATHENS • TOKYO • MILAN • MADRID
PRAGUE • WARSAW • BUDAPEST • AUCKLAND

Recycling programs
for this product may
not exist in your area.

ISBN-13: 978-0-373-78427-1

HERE COMES THE GROOM

ABOUT THE AUTHOR

New Zealander Karina Bliss is a winner of Romance Writers of America's coveted Golden Heart award for unpublished writers and her 2006 Superromance debut, *Mr. Imperfect,* won a Romantic Book of the Year award in Australia. She's currently writing her ninth romance for the Harlequin Superromance line on the next hero in her SAS series—Ross Coltrane, who features in *Here Comes the Groom.* The former journalist lives with her husband and son north of Auckland. Visit her on the web at www.karinabliss.com, where Karina runs regular draws for her backlist and also posts excerpts of upcoming books.

Books by Karina Bliss

HARLEQUIN SUPERROMANCE

To every reader who has emailed
to say they've enjoyed one of my books.
You make my day.

Acknowledgments

Many thanks to Kate Gordon and Audrey Walker
(via Pamela Gervai) for their insight into farming.
In the novel, I refer to a book called
Contented Dementia written by Oliver James.
I found it an excellent resource
and highly recommend it.

CHAPTER ONE

IT WAS AT THE POINT her bar pickup started whispering the naughty things he wanted to do to her that Jocelyn Swann realized that, while she was drunk, she wasn't drunk enough.

Rubbing the tickle out of her ear, she planted an encouraging kiss on Tony-the-Corporate-High-Flyer's sexy mouth and said, "Hold that thought, hotshot." Wriggling seductively out of the circular booth, she threaded past the ladies' room and doubled back to the dimly lit bar.

One more shooter should do it—silence the disapproving voice that kept whining, "This is not a good idea."

"Shut up," she muttered. The bartender, a student who looked as out of place in the hotel's funky bar as she felt, looked up. "Not you... Sorry, Phil." Leaning over, she patted his scrawny shoulder.

His bespectacled gaze instinctively dropped to the girls, nicely displayed by Jo's push-up bra and low-cut chiffon top. She froze on a sudden upwelling of grief, then laughed and shimmied them. "Pretty good, huh? One of my best features, I'm told."

Phil averted his gaze. "Um…yeah, sure… What would you like?"

"A sublime sexual experience that I'll remember the rest of my life," she confided. "But right now, another Jägerbomb will do."

"Okaaay," said Phil slowly. "On your room tab again, Ms. Swann? Eight oh One, wasn't it?"

"Thanks, mate." He filled a tumbler with Red Bull, then dropped in a shot glass of Jägermeister. Jo watched the red-brown liqueur billow into the gold and told herself it didn't look like a blood spill because that would be morbid and tonight was all about having fun with a capital *F.*

"Got the time?" she asked. "Hard to tell in this place." Plush and windowless with pods of circular white booths, Bar None was an artful contrast of shadows and soft blue spotlights that spilled nowhere useful. Jo had to squint to sign for her drink.

"Ten o'clock."

"Guess this better be my last." Picking up her cocktail, Jo knocked it back with a grimace. The anise flavor wasn't as nice as it had been two shots ago. "Nothing by mouth after midnight," she commented. "But you're the med student, Phil. A couple of buffer hours would be sensible, right?"

His eyes bugged. "You're drinking...the night before surgery?" He snatched her glass. "You shouldn't touch alcohol for at least forty-eight hours before."

Does the joy never end? Then the Jägerbomb dropped its alcohol load, the song changed to Ben Harper's version of "Sexual Healing" and Jo started to laugh. "I should care but I don't. No, don't nag, Phil, your future patients won't like it."

Riding the buzz, Jo danced back to her prey. He was engrossed in a call—how cutely corporate—cell to one ear, hand over the other. As Jo did a last hip swivel she heard "I love you, too," and stopped mid twist. *Please let that be his mother.*

Tony glanced up, caught sight of her and his face said it all. Married.

Her stomach plummeted. "You despicable, lying worm, you told me you were single."

Cutting off the call, he pocketed his cell. "Jo, I—"

"Forget it. I've just wasted two precious hours on you...hours I'll never ever get back." Her voice shook. "I haven't even got the time to make you suffer...now get out!"

Tony didn't need to be told twice. When he'd

gone, Jo sank into the booth, rested her elbows on the table and cradled her spinning head until her nausea subsided. Married! Thank God she'd found out before she slept with him. There was a jug of water on the table. She slopped some into Tony's empty glass, wiped the rim with a cocktail napkin and drank it, desperately scanning the bar for new prospects. Too old, too young, too thin, too slick.

Dammit, the alcohol wasn't just for Dutch courage—it was supposed to be lowering her standards.

An hour later, Jo was having her neck nuzzled by Brad-the-Banker. "You're gorgeous," he murmured. "I can't believe my luck meeting you tonight."

Jo closed her eyes, the better to assess his skills—not bad—then quickly opened them again. The dizziness receded, replaced by handsome blondness.

Brad's knuckles brushed the outside of her breast. "And you're so sexy, I—" Ribald male laughter burst from an adjacent table. He frowned. "Yobos."

"Who cares?" Jo planted his palm against her curves. "Tell me I'm sexy again."

Brad's brown eyes darkened and he smiled, spreading his fingers to encompass her breast. Leaning closer, he opened his mouth to speak.

"Hey…sexy."

Jo jerked her head around to see who the deep, masculine drawl belonged to. "Dan!"

Her instinctive delight at seeing her oldest friend subsided into embarrassment as he took in her slutty top, the scarlet lipstick and Brad's intimate caress. Grabbing her pickup's fingers, she tried to act casual. "What are you doing here?" She enunciated her words carefully so Dan wouldn't know how drunk she was. "Weren't you on a surf trip down south?"

Amused, he lifted his teal-blue eyes from her pushed-up cleavage. "No swell… When I heard you were on your own in the Big Smoke, I figured you could use some company." Dan grinned, shrugging his wide shoulders. "Guess I figured wrong." Turning to Brad, he held out a hand. "Dan Jansen…I grew up with Jo in Beacon Bay."

Brad tried to disentangle from Jo's restraining grip. "Brad Wilson. I met her tonight."

"Rea-a-ally?" Dan drawled and she felt the beginning of a blush. "Relax, Swannie," he added. "What happens in Auckland stays in Auckland."

The two men shook hands and Jo squirmed as she watched Brad deliver a bone-crusher. Dan responded by stroking the other man's knuckle with his thumb. Brad couldn't release fast enough. Her best friend looked at her. *You can't be serious.*

"Brad is an investment banker," she said desperately.

"Impressive," said Dan.

Brad studied Dan, who was wearing a polo shirt over dress jeans, then he leaned back, crossed his legs in their expensive suit pants and flung an arm across Jo's shoulders. "And what do you do when you're not surfing?"

"I'm a soldier."

"Really?" Brad's eyebrows rose in surprise. Dan might be one of the world's most lethal combatants, but projecting a self-effacing mildness was a crucial part of their skill set. The guy looked at his disheveled brown hair. "I thought all you guys had crew cuts."

"I've been on a month's leave."

"Nice for some," said Brad, unaware that Dan had earned it after a six-month deployment in Afghanistan. He smiled down at Jo. "I can't remember the last time I took a break."

Why did corporates think being a workaholic was a turn-on?

"Yeah," Dan said sympathetically, "rebuilding credibility must involve really long hours."

Brad frowned. "The credit crisis wasn't a picnic for the banking industry, either." Jo began to fidget. This guy was really pompous. She had to get him out of here and into bed before her friend put her off him completely.

Dan sat with the air of a man prepared to enjoy himself. "I'd love to hear your take on that."

Jo nudged her pickup. "Except we were about to leave."

Brad looked down her cleavage. "Whatever you say."

"Is this the part where I ask your intentions, Bradley?" Dan was still smiling but not with his eyes. Brad removed his arm from Jo's shoulders.

She put it back. "Relax, Jansen. I know who I'm doing."

"Yeah? How much have you had to drink?"

Jo turned to Brad with a flirtatious smile. "I need a quick word with my overprotective friend. Don't go anywhere."

"She's been this bossy since first grade," Dan confided. "Hope you enjoy being the girl."

"Such a kidder." Jo dragged Dan out of the booth and out of earshot. "Look, I know you're worried that I'm drunk and being taken advantage of, but trust me it's the other way around."

Dan looked skeptical, and impatiently Jo jiggled her up-thrust cleavage. "Isn't it obvious I dressed to get laid?"

"Can you quit bouncing those things in front of me?" He sounded irritated. "You're making me feel like a pervert."

"That's because all guys are shallow."

"Yeah, and you're only interested in Brad's personality."

"My point is," she said, sticking doggedly to it, "quit with the third degree. I'm not chasing blue-chip investment here. Bad—I mean, *Brad* and I are all about mutual-asset stripping and quick returns."

"You wouldn't have sex with him if you weren't drunk though, would you?"

"Tracy," said Jo. "Mandy… Shall I go on? Angie."

He held up his hands. "Fine, you've made your point, I'll say goodbye and disappear."

"Thank you." They returned to the booth. It was empty. Jo resisted the urge to check under the table. "You've scared him off."

"He could be in the men's room."

"Go check."

"You're not serious."

She gave him a panicky push. "Go check."

But he came out alone, shrugging his broad shoulders. Jo swallowed hard. That was it then, her last chance gone. And Dan thought it was funny, she could tell.

"Sorry."

"No, you're not." To her horror she could feel her eyes welling.

Dan's jaw dropped. "Jo?"

Scowling, she blinked, but that only sent two tears trickling down her cheek.

"Hell, I'm sorry. I didn't realize this mattered." Dan wiped her tears away with his thumb. "I'll hunt him down for you."

Her laugh was half sob. "Because that'll rekindle the romance."

"C'mon, mate." He put an arm around her. "You know he's not worth this."

"I'm not crying for him." Suddenly exhausted, she leaned her head against his shoulder. "I'm crying for…" Jo straightened, forced a smile. "Hell, I don't know why I'm crying. Must be the alcohol."

He searched her face. "You only get drunk when you're in trouble."

Jo closed her eyes. "I feel sick."

"Oh, God, hang on." *It worked.* He steered her toward the ladies' room. She'd thrown up on him before—at her sixth birthday party when they'd been jumping on the trampoline after Jo had eaten too many candies.

"I think I can make it to my room. On my own."

"I'll walk you."

Not safe from interrogation yet, then. But she

was glad of his support as they walked across the foyer. The black-and-white checked tiles kept moving. The hotel receptionist darted a curious glance at Dan as Jo asked for her key. "We're just friends," she clarified.

"Of course," the girl answered in disbelief, her tone envious. She passed the key over.

Certainly Dan was a looker; even knowing him forever, Jo could appreciate that. But she also knew all that warm, sexy charm was a mask. Behind it, he held himself separate. Like Jo did. Even now he was clearly thinking about something else.

"I expected the hotel to be full of delegates," he said and Jo dropped her key. "Doesn't your publishers' conference start tomorrow?"

"Conference?" said the receptionist.

"This isn't the venue." Hastily Jo bent to pick up her key and nearly fell over. "I wanted a quieter hotel." She steered Dan away from reception. "Why *are* you in Auckland? I thought you were back in Beacon Bay."

"I've been recalled. We're going over the hill within the next few days."

SAS speak for overseas deployment. Only Dan knew whether it was an exercise or for real. But Jo was a journalist, she kept an eye on the news feeds. And it was no secret that the United States had formally asked for New

Zealand's SAS to be sent to Afghanistan. "The Middle East?"

His face shuttered. "I can't tell you that."

"How long?"

"Six months."

Jo was torn between anxiety for his safety and a sense of reprieve. She didn't enjoy lying to him. "What did Maxine say?" His girlfriend didn't cope well with his job.

"Let's just say I got more than one set of marching orders today."

Jo stopped halfway to the elevators. "Dan, I'm sorry."

He laughed, propelling her forward. "It's okay, mate, I'm not heartbroken."

"You should be. Maxine was a keeper."

"What a shame that I'm already engaged—to you."

She snorted. Four years earlier when Jo had broken up with Chris, a guy she'd hoped was the One, and was fretting that she'd never get the large family she wanted, Dan had promised to marry her if they were both still single at thirty-three. They'd signed the contract on a beer mat. "You only use that as an excuse with other women."

"And very useful it's been, too."

They reached the elevator and he pushed the call button. The shiny chrome doors reflected a

redheaded bimbo in a filmy, low-cut top clinging to him. It took Jo a moment to recognize
herself. On the other hand she'd been having
out-of-body experiences for ten days—ever
since she'd heard the news from her doctor.
Releasing Dan, Jo hugged herself.

He glanced at her. "You feeling sick
again?"

"I'm all right," she said numbly.

The elevator's doors swished open and its two
occupants sprang guiltily apart. A bride and
groom in their early twenties, still dotted with
confetti.

"It's okay," Dan reminded them, "you're married now."

The bride giggled. "Hey, that's right." She
shifted her veil to make room for them, but they
still had to skirt her Cinderella dress.

"Congratulations," said Jo, pressing the button
for her floor.

"Thanks," replied the groom as he turned
an adoring gaze on his bride. The elevator
started with a jolt. Jo fell back against Dan and
he steadied her. The groom murmured into the
bride's ear. "Dare you…" And laughing, she
stood on tiptoe and kissed him passionately.

Jo fanned out her top and stared at the num-
bers flashing on the panel, 2…3…4. She'd
wanted that so badly tonight. Not love—at

thirty-one she'd lost faith in that—but lust. She would have settled for lust. Brad might have been an arrogant ass but he knew what a woman wanted to hear—that she was desirable—and he could have made her forget.

The elevator stopped at six. The happy couple disembarked, leaving behind their heat and their pheromones. Jo gazed after them wistfully.

Dan leaned over her shoulder to jab the door-close button, and his warm breath stirred her hair. Slowly turning her head, Jo stared at him as he moved to her right, giving her more room. He and Maxine had broken up. Maybe it was a sign?

She dragged her eyes to the flashing panel. Yeah, a sign you're drunk! You don't risk a twenty-seven-year friendship by suggesting a one-night stand. Except…what she *might* lose suddenly didn't seem important weighed against what she *might* lose tomorrow.

"You sure you're okay, Jo? You look pale."

"Relax, I'm not going to throw up on you."

"Thank God for that."

"Here we are." Dan led the way to her room, taking her key when Jo fumbled it and opened the door.

"Come in," she invited him. "We've hardly talked. Help yourself to a drink from the mini-bar, I won't be a minute."

Staggering into the bathroom, Jo splashed water on her face, she finger-combed her disheveled hair and left the bathroom, licking her glossy lips. *I need a memory hot enough to last me a lifetime.*

She found Dan pouring boiling water into two mugs. "I've made coffee," he said, over his shoulder. "You probably need it."

"Sounds good." Her heart was beating so fast he must hear it. Jo looped her arms around his waist and laid her face against his back.

"Maybe you'd better lie down," he said, adding sugar and milk, "if you can't stand up by yourself."

Frustrated, Jo released him. "Dan, turn around."

He picked up the mugs and turned, pulling them up over her head in the nick of time.

"What the…" Stepping between the outstretched mugs, she yanked his face down to hers. Dan stiffened. "Jo, don't—"

She kissed him, stifling his protests with her tongue.

It was odd kissing someone she loved platonically, odd and way too much like a science experiment. Although… Dan wrenched his mouth away and said in a tight voice, "Step away, before you get burned."

"Wow, you really think you're that good?"

then she realized he was still holding the mugs outstretched, and hot coffee was dripping over his fingers and splattering onto the cream carpet.

She sobered, real fast. "Dan…"

"Just get out of the goddamn way, Jo."

He dumped the mugs on the bedside table and disappeared into the bathroom where she heard him turn on the faucet. For a moment, Jo stood in abject humiliation before wrapping herself in a dressing gown and following him. He had his fingers under a stream of cold water.

"Dan," she choked. "I'm sorry."

"You bloody should be!" His eyes met hers in the mirror. "Where's your brain, Jo?"

"It was only a one-off," she protested. "I might be drunk and stupid but I'm not that drunk and stupid."

His mouth twitched. "This isn't even about me, is it?" She shook her head and relief softened his features. "So what…the ticking clock again?"

It took her a moment to realize he was talking about her desire to have children. She dropped her gaze. "It's silly, I know."

"You're not even thirty-two."

"You're right," she said. *Only thirty-one. It wasn't fair.* Jo started to cry, she couldn't help it.

With an oath, Dan turned off the tap and pulled her into a hug.

"You're an idiot, Swannie," he said roughly. "You've still got plenty of time."

Jo cried harder.

"You'll be glad I turned you down when you sober up. And we'll forget about this."

"Okay," she sobbed. It was so good to be held by someone who actually cared about her.

"I'll find you a goddamn husband when I get home."

"Okay." It was easier to agree with him.

He gave her a shake. "Quit crying now."

"Okay." Jo made an effort and wiped her eyes with the corner of his shirt. "Um…Dan?" she sniffed.

"Yeah, mate."

"I'm going to be sick now."

"Oh, great."

CHAPTER TWO

Twelve months later

HIS STALKER LEAPED OUT of the moon-
less dark.

Only a panting yip seconds before front paws
slammed into Dan's chest made him drop the
knife in time. He caught the border collie in
his arms, a furry mass of squirming, whining
affection. "Goddamn it, Blue!"

Heart still climbing his throat, Dan dropped
to his knees on the rough driveway leading to
the farmhouse and tightened his hold. "Don't
try and ambush a soldier." *Especially not SAS.*
A sloppy, rough tongue licked his unshaven
jaw.

Even in the pitch dark, the New Zealand landscape smelled different from Afghanistan—pine
and lush pasture instead of arid desert and rock.
Life, not death.

Pushing the ecstatic animal away, Dan felt
for his knife on the loose stones, then shoved
it to the bottom of his backpack. It wasn't like

him to get disoriented like this. Still crouching, he covered his face with his hands, breathing deeply. *Hey, folks, I accidentally killed the dog thinking he was al Qaeda, but otherwise I'm perfectly normal.*

Blue rolled into him, knocking Dan onto his ass. Sharp stones digging through his worn jeans, he struggled to see the dog and laughed. Still on his back, wriggling, the collie's jaw stretched wide in a canine grin.

"What the hell are you doing here anyway, eh, boy?" Leaning forward, he scratched Blue's exposed belly. "You're supposed to be living in town with the parents... Yeah, well, I'm happy to see you, too. Now go on." He pushed the dog to its feet, rose to his own. "Lead the way home." Blue tore off into the night.

Reshouldering his pack, Dan followed the faint sound of dislodged stones, the sonic trigger that had caused him to pull his knife in the first place. He'd forgotten the impenetrable blackness of a cloudy country night, the sense of total isolation. In early May there was a crispness to the air, the first breath of impending winter.

The moon broke through. There was enough light now to make out the dog's pricked ears as Blue waited for him to catch up. Farther up the track, the empty farmhouse came into view, white clapboard, corrugated iron roof, and a low-pitch verandah with pegs and shelves for wet weather gear and gum boots. No cow manure would ever be tracked through his mother's kitchen.

He could tell she didn't live here anymore, though. The porch needed sweeping and the doormat was caked in mud. This place was his now, at least until he decided whether to buy into the farm.

He slid his hand between the second and third step for the spare key, still on a hook under the porch. Some things didn't change. He found comfort in that. Unlocking the door he stepped inside.

"Move one inch, you thieving bastard," said a gruff voice, "and I'll pepper your ass with steel shot." There was the sound of a double-barrel snapping shut.

Dan grinned. "Is that any way to welcome your firstborn home?"

HIS FATHER POURED THEM both a whiskey to steady their nerves. "Creeping in at midnight." Herman pushed the shot glass across the kitchen table, his thick gray hair tufted from sleep. "Who the hell do you think you are, Cinderella?"

"Hitchhikers take rides when they can." Dan had been on operational deployment for six months in rugged, mountainous terrain.

Given his haggard appearance, he considered himself lucky to have been picked up at all. "I had to walk the last five kilometers from the turnoff."

"With that pack? You should have called me."

It hadn't occurred to him; he was so used to self-sufficiency. And the backpack weighed a fraction of the twenty-plus pounds he usually carried. Picking up his whiskey, Dan looked curiously at his old man. "What are you doing here anyway? I thought you and Mom moved to town two months ago." And it looked like it. The kitchen held only an old table and two mismatched chairs. One mug in the sink. A small fridge.

Herman started toying with his glass. "I wasn't happy leaving this place vacant—isolated the way it is—so I stay over weeknights. I'm still working on the farm every day with Rob. It's more convenient to sleep here." The nineteen-year-old farm hand rented the old cottage at the other end of the property, and had been looking after the farm dogs since their move to town.

The amber liquid burned a path down Dan's throat, warming all the cold places. "Town's only a fifteen-minute drive away. Hardly a commute. And Rob's only a few acres over."

"Now you sound like your mother." Herman went and got the whiskey bottle. "Anyway, it was only until you came home."

"So I've been holding up your retirement plans?" He hadn't been home in almost a year, spending his leave with one of his younger twin sisters—Viv—in New York.

"Not my plans, son—hers. Personally I'm in no hurry to turn into an old dodderer."

"At sixty-five? Hardly." Herman Jansen was still a vital, handsome man, with a full head of hair, piercing blue eyes and a strong Dutch jaw. Popeye, as his three children affectionately referred to him. "Isn't retirement about having freedom? To travel, play golf…" Dan grinned. "Spend quality time with the grandkids."

His father shuddered. Privately, Herman called Tilly, his granddaughter—offspring of the domesticated twin—Attila.

"I can rejoin the SAS," Dan offered. "Mom need never know I was here."

"Hell, no. I'd give up six farms to keep you home safe." Herman stopped, cleared his throat, but his voice was gruff when he added, "Your aunt and uncle are still taking it very hard. When I think—"

"Dad."

For a long moment they stared at each other,

then Herman nodded and refilled their glasses. "All right, son," he said. "All right."

He'd been wrong; his father could look old. Dan cleared his own throat. "How's this trial handover going to work?"

"I thought I should hold the reins for another few weeks...just until you settle in. And I promised Rob a holiday as soon as you came back."

He wasn't fooled by his father's nonchalance. Giving up a farm you'd run for forty years wasn't something to be hurried. Neither was taking one over. "I was hoping you'd hang around. I'll need a refresher course."

Though he'd made a point of keeping up with farming innovations, Dan had been off the land for thirteen years. Managing a 550-hectare property that ran over three thousand sheep and four hundred beef cattle wasn't a walk in the park.

If it had been, he wouldn't have been interested. "Besides, you've got to make sure I'm competent, if Mom's going to be spending money renting villas in Tuscany."

Herman gave a resigned grunt. "She's been making me take Italian lessons," he grumbled. "*Accettate carte di credito?* Do you accept credit cards?"

Dan laughed.

"It's not funny, son. Back me up on a handover period or she'll have me on a plane before you can say *arrivederci*."

"Relax, you've got at least twenty-four days. Mom won't go overseas before my wedding."

"What?" His father nearly dropped his whiskey. "You're getting married? Danny, you making fun?"

Pulling an invitation out of his pack, Dan slid it across the table. "Herman, I've never been more serious about anything in my life." He knocked back his drink in one burning gulp.

EVERY MORNING FOR THE past year when Jo woke up she sang the same silly tune under her breath. "I'm A-live, A-wake, A-lert, Enthussss-iass-tic."

The friend's preschooler who'd taught her the song performed it with matching actions. "I'm a-live—" tap head "—a-wake—" tap eyes "—a-lert—" tap shoulders "—enthusss-iass-tic!" big star jump.

On a bad day Jo forced herself to do the actions; lately she'd simply sung it under her breath. Today, her thirty-third birthday, she ditched the song altogether and set her watch for an extra five minutes in bed.

It wasn't a bed that invited a lie-in, being narrow and single with a fluorescent lime-green duvet cover that didn't just draw the eye but imploded it. Ten months ago when Jo first moved back to the house she'd grown up in, she'd brought her own double bed and dumped her laminated school certificates and surf lifesaving medals in the bedside drawer. Her grandmother had gotten agitated so Jo returned everything to the way it was. Fortunately Nan hadn't noticed the New Kids on the Block poster still missing from the wardrobe door.

A shaft of sun striped the edge of her pillow; she laid her hand on it. In late autumn it had little heat but it didn't matter. For the first time in months she saw light at the end of the tunnel, saw solutions and possibilities. She saw her old self. On a surge of optimism Jo stretched her arms over her head, relishing the pull of joints and muscle. I'm back, she thought.

Her watch beeped. Flinging off the blankets she got up and padded across the hall to the old-fashioned bathroom. With a longing look at the claw-foot bath, she settled for a quick shower in the tiny stall installed after Nan had flooded the bathroom for the second time.

She was towel-drying her hair when the handle rattled on the door. Jo just had time to reposition the towel before her eighty-five-year old grandmother bowled in, dressed in a red quilted dressing gown, her best pearls and a gardening hat.

"Good morning, Nan! Remember we knock first?" *My fault for forgetting to lock the door.*

"I used to change your diapers. Now, what did I come in here for?" Rosemary tapped her frowning forehead with soft, wrinkled fingers.

"To wish me happy birthday, but I'll be out in a minute." Gently she turned her grandmother toward the door.

"Oh, yes, I'm making boiled eggs for your breakfast."

Uh-oh. "I'll be right down." Jo scrambled into the suit she'd laid out for her meeting today—tailored gray trousers and jacket, teamed with a feminine ruffle-front shirt in pale apricot chiffon and matching shoes, higher than she normally wore. Hastily finger-combing her short auburn curls she hurried downstairs to the kitchen, which, at the back of the house, overlooked an autumn-shabby vegetable garden and orchard.

Nan was spooning coffee into the teapot. "Sit down, darling, everything's under control."

"Excellent." Turning off the glowing stove element, Jo kissed Rosemary's wrinkled cheek. "But I need a teaspoon for my boiled egg."

When her grandmother turned to find one, she rinsed the coffee out of the teapot, dropped in a couple of teabags and added the boiling water.

Nan paused in the midst of opening drawers. "What am I looking for, again?"

"A teaspoon."

"Oh, yes, here you are." Nan shooed her toward the table. "Now go eat before it gets cold."

The egg sat in a rooster eggcup on a fine bone-china plate beside a loaf of bread still in the bag. Tentatively, Jo fractured the shell. Transparent egg white seeped through the crack. "Nan, I forgot the milk."

En route to the table, Rosemary turned back to the fridge. Quickly Jo opened the cracked shell, dumped the raw egg into a paper napkin and folded it over, then replaced the shell in the eggcup.

Head in the depths of the fridge, Rosemary called. "What am I looking for?"

"The milk."

Retrieving the carton, her grandmother joined her. "Goodness, you were hungry."

Jo poured the tea. "So, what's in your diary today?"

Nan pulled it from the pocket of her dressing gown. "Now," she patted her gardening hat, "where are my glasses?"

"I'll find them." Jo searched the most likely places first.

"They're hardly going to be in the oven, dear," said Rosemary, amused.

"Of course not. I don't know where my head's at this morning." Jo found them in the breadbox.

Nan put them on, looping the silver chain around her neck, and peered at the diary that reminded her where she was in place and time. "Alec and Elaine for morning tea. And Polly's coming…you know, Jocelyn, I really think you should speak to that girl, she does so little housework."

"Well, she's more of a companion than a cleaning lady."

But Rosemary wasn't paying attention. Head tilted, she listened to something Jo couldn't hear with an intent expression. "I think you'll have to wake your grandfather."

Reaching across the table, Jo took her grandmother's hand. "Pops passed away years ago."

"What?" Breaking Jo's hold, Rosemary pulled her dressing gown closer. "He had a stroke at work.… Yes, I remember now.…" Behind the glasses, her eyes were suddenly sharp. "I'm in the kitchen," she said deliberately, "eating breakfast with my granddaughter." Her gaze fixed on the calendar, the date decorated with bright stars. "It's May 2, Jocelyn's birthday... darling, why didn't you remind me? Today she's..."

"Thirty-three," Jo prompted.

"So old!" Rosemary exclaimed. "What does that make me...? No, don't tell me. Some things *are* better forgotten." She picked up her diary and read it, lips moving silently. Early in her illness Nan had written in it religiously. Now it was usually Polly or Jo who filled in the details. "Oh, good. I bought you a birthday present." Relief smoothed the angular planes of her face and softened the blue-gray eyes Jo had inherited. "It's in the dresser drawer."

Jo fetched the small box and opened it. A pair of diamond earrings.

"Oh, Nan, they're beautiful."

Her grandmother removed her glasses, letting them fall on the chain. "Polly helped me choose them. You know, Jocelyn, I really think you should speak to that girl, she does so little housework."

The "girl" came into the kitchen at that moment, a large, round woman in her fifties, with the no-nonsense briskness of her former profession as a charge nurse. Pocketing her key, she looked at the teapot. "Tea hot? I'm gasping."

Nan sent Jo a pointed glance, which Polly caught. "Uh-oh. I'm a servant today, am I?" she said cheerfully. Taking off her coat, she hung it with her bag on a peg by the back door. "You might want to get dressed, Rosemary. We've got visitors this morning."

"Visitors?" Nan put on her glasses and checked her diary. "Alec and Elaine for morning tea. Jocelyn, why didn't you remind me?" She left the kitchen abruptly.

"Well, birthday girl," said Polly, pouring herself some tea. "How are you celebrating?"

"Birthdays are overrated." Jo took her plate to the dishwasher.

"As I thought. Well, I'm taking Nan home with me as your birthday present, so plan on going out tonight and having some fun."

"No, Polly, you already do enough. Besides, I should spend it with Nan."

"Rosemary won't remember and you need a break. When did you last have time to yourself?" Mug in one hand, Polly helped clear the table with the other. "All your waking hours are spent either running the *Chronicle* or looking after your grandmother."

"My two great loves." Knowing where this was heading, Jo disappeared into the laundry, where she transferred an overnight load from the washing machine into the dryer.

Polly followed her. "Honey, this isn't what she wanted for you."

"We're not discussing this on my birthday. Anyway, haven't you noticed? I'm bouncing with energy these days."

"Uh-huh," Polly said skeptically. "Living on adrenaline overload more like." The older woman went and got Jo's briefcase. "Go out tonight," she ordered her. "I don't want to see a light on this hill until past eleven, you hear me? And don't think I won't be watching."

Flashlight, then. "Yes, ma'am. I'll check in later." Jo went out to the mailbox. Bills mostly. Which reminded her that she'd forgotten the earrings. She'd return them on the way to work. She had the same arrangement with all the stores. Nan could buy anything she wanted; Jo would return it and the retailer got a discount on their *Chronicle* advertising.

Walking back into the house, she turned over a square silver envelope and smiled as she recognized Dan's scrawl. He never forgot to send a birthday card, which depending on where he was stationed, would sometimes arrive weeks late. Checking the postmark she blinked. Auckland. Yesterday. He was already in the country? She ripped it open, looked at the cover and laughed out loud.

"What's funny?" Polly poked her head out from the laundry.

"Private joke. See you tomorrow." Jo picked up the jeweler's box from the kitchen table and left the house remembering her conversation with him last month when he'd phoned from Kabul.

"You're coming up for thirty-three, Swannie. We still on for that wedding?"

His troop mates' deaths had hit him hard; it was such a relief to hear him joking again.

"Relax, you're off the hook. To quote Katharine Hepburn, 'Why give up the admiration of many men for the criticism of one?'"

"What about all those kids you wanted?"

"The *Chronicle*'s the only baby I need."

Dan snorted in disbelief. After all, she'd talked about having kids forever. "So I thought I'd use the beer mat we signed our pledge on as the wedding invitation."

"Really? You've still got that?" Jo played along. "Well, I don't want to be sued for breach of promise so I guess I'll have to marry you. But let's make the invitations tasteful. I'm thinking a picture of a bride hauling her groom to the altar by the hair…maybe a camouflage background as a nod to your military background."

"And the text?"

"Hey, this is a partnership," she joked. "It's your turn to come up with ideas."

"Okay, mate, you leave it all to me."

She looked at the wedding invitation now and laughed again because he'd replicated every detail. Opening it, Jo skimmed over Dan's name to the bride's. As expected. Hers.

The day was shaping up to be fun.

CHAPTER THREE

IT STARTED RAINING as Jo drove her VW Polo down the rolling hills that protected Beacon Bay—squally autumn rain with sun laced through it. The harbor town sprawled around a sideways bite out of the land—estuary on one side of the peninsula, sea on the other. When Jo's grandfather had settled here, he'd been the first in the valley.

Now it was a mass of roofs and aerials, the houses increasing in size and grandeur the closer they got to the water. Oceanside, the sea was a sullen gray—no swell today for the surfers to skip work or school for. A couple of fishing trawlers dotted the horizon.

Checking her cell, Jo saw she had seven messages already. Well, that was to be expected. The *Chronicle* hit letterboxes on Friday. Which meant Monday was complaints day. She started returning calls on her hands-free speakerphone.

"No, Bob, I don't think I quoted you out of context. Before you were elected you said you'd fight to prevent developers making Beacon Bay a weekend playground for Aucklanders. Now you're saying the only way to beat the recession is to make it easier for developers." Jo maneuvered the car into a tight parking space outside the jewelers. "Well, that's an interesting suggestion but I don't think my body contorts that way."

She returned the jewelry, dialing the next number as soon as she was back in the car. "You approved the ad, John. If you don't like the font now it's printed, you still have to pay for it.

"Clive, I'm sorry you're disappointed but I did tell you last month that we'd have to temporarily decrease our funding of the surf club." For a moment Jo considered telling the disappointed fundraiser how much it pained her to do this, but stopped herself.

When her grandfather's death put her at the helm of his business at the age of twenty-three she'd evolved strategies to cope. Always act like you know what you're doing. Be decisive. Never apologize; never explain. At the time she couldn't afford to show weakness, not when so many jobs depended on her.

She still couldn't afford it.

"I hope the *Chronicle* will be in a position to increase sponsorship in another couple of months," she said brusquely. Unfortunately challenges in her personal life had coincided with the economic downturn. The paper's revenue had suffered. But four months ago, Polly had increased her hours, freeing Jo to rebuild her neglected business. Each month's figures were improving.

Kevin was the only person in the office when she arrived at seven-thirty. They'd started at the *Chronicle* the same year, Jo twenty and fresh from a degree in journalism; and Kevin, forty-five, a disillusioned English teacher from the city looking for a lifestyle change.

Thirteen years later, the paper's chief sub still looked like a scholar with his rounded shoulders, an intellectual's deep groove between his bushy eyebrows and a total indifference to fashion. With the weather cooling, he wore socks under his Birkenstocks.

He was doing the crossword and looked up over his reading glasses. "You kept this mighty quiet," he said and tossed the wedding invitation across his desk.

"I'll kill him," Jo replied without heat. Of course Dan would make the most of this. "It's a joke, Kev. Isn't that obvious from the picture and the camouflage background?"

"I did wonder," he confessed, "but you two have a warped sense of humor. And the text is played straight." Jo flipped the wedding invite open and read it through for the first time.

"That boy has no imagination," she complained. "You'd think he could have added a few jokes... Anyway, enough distraction. I need to prepare for this meeting with CommLink."

Kev wrote *temsik* in one of the crossword squares before looking up anxiously. "And you're definitely saying no? Even if they make you a brilliant offer?"

"Even if they make me a brilliant offer." She rearranged the upside-down letters in her head. *Kismet.* "I'll say they caught me in a weak moment, but on reflection I couldn't possible sell the *Chronicle.*" She'd expected relief but Kev was still frowning at her. "What?"

"That wasn't a weak moment—it was a rip in the fabric of society. You, the people's champion, selling out to a soulless corporate conglomerate that only cares about maximizing profit? It's like Michael Moore joining the gun lobby. Okay, you had that shoulder injury and Rosemary's illness grinding you down but—"

"Kev," she interrupted him. "Can you please move on?"

When CommLink came a-wooing she'd been under intense emotional pressure and desperate for a relief valve. Unable to do more than pay lip service to her business, it had seemed sensible to investigate options, particularly with the economy playing havoc with sales.

"I don't think you should tell them you had a weak moment, either," he added. "Maybe I should come with you."

"No." Jo stared him down. "I've got systems in place to manage Nan's dementia and my shoulder's fully recovered. I promise, no more weak moments."

There was a piercing shriek from the door and Delwyn rushed over, waving the wedding invitation she held in her manicured hand, her acrylic nails flashing. Jo's heart sank. Exactly how many invitations had Dan sent out?

"Oh. My. God!" Her brown eyes sparkled. "Jo, how could you not have told me this! I could have given you my countdown-to-conjugals calendar."

The bubbly young sales rep was getting married in July. For the past year, she'd been planning her nuptials with the kind of single-minded intensity normally associated with the invasion of small countries.

As usual Delwyn didn't wait for a response. "It's been so long since you dated I'd even started to wonder if you'd changed teams. Especially when you got your hair cut so short."

Flicking her glossy brown hair back from her

face, Delwyn frowned as Kev frantically shook his head.

"Did I say something wrong?"

SHAKER'S BAR & GRILL was a Beacon Bay institution on the estuary, only a sprawl of lawn separating it from the sea.

The yeasty mimosa of local specialty beer all but permeated the walls, but on a cold day nothing beat a table near the fire gazing out through the salt-kissed glass to the seabirds hovering over the broad sweep of estuary.

Having spent the morning fending off wedding congratulations, Jo was in no mood to appreciate the view. Dan was so going to pay for this.

About to go in, she saw her ex Chris Boyle getting out of a Mercedes with CommLink's financial controller, Grant. The sight dismayed her, not because she felt uncomfortable around an old boyfriend, but because if the company's bigwig was here, CommLink had wanted the *Chronicle* badly. Well, it couldn't be helped.

Grant looked nervous as they approached. Sandy-haired and shy, he and Jo had gone to school together. He'd introduced her to Chris at Jo's first publishing conference. Maybe he was feeling the awkwardness of that now. Giving him a reassuring smile, she held out her hand to Chris. "What's it been…four years?"

"And you're still the same." His smiling gaze slid over her slim curves.

When she'd finally realized his self-assurance-cloaked arrogance and broken it off—a first for Chris—he'd retaliated by called her a ball-breaker. "Afraid so," she said genially. "Shall we go in, gentlemen?"

Grant raised his water glass as soon as they were seated. "So, congratulations! I got your wedding invitation this morning."

This bloody joke was losing its humor fast. Jo hesitated. She didn't want to explain in front of Chris who'd inspired her pact with Dan in the first place. "Thanks," she said and retreated behind her menu. She'd tell Grant privately when she got the chance. "The chicken pie is particularly good."

"I always thought you and Dan belonged together," continued Grant earnestly. "Even at school he was the one person you couldn't man—" Realizing he was about to insult his boss, he picked up his menu. "The chicken pie you say?"

Manage. Jo finished his sentence. As affable and easygoing as Dan was, he went his own way, not just with her but with everybody. And she'd never worked out how he did it. Which annoyed her. And made her laugh. The wedding invitation extended a long tradition.

"So, Chris," she changed the subject again, "how many kids do you have now?" He'd married six months after they'd broken up. Someone sweet and compliant.

"Two and another on the way." Proudly, he pulled out pictures of his girls and became a much nicer man. "I remember you always wanted three yourself. You and Dan planning a family?"

"Still under discussion." Maybe a bathroom break would kill this subject. "Would you two excuse me for a minute?"

Ten minutes later as Jo returned through the lunchtime crowd, she heard a familiar drawl. Abruptly, she stopped. For a moment she couldn't see him, then a gap opened around the bar and Dan came into view, talking to the manager, Anton.

The desert sun had tanned his skin and lightened his hair to the streaked gold it used to be when they were kids. You could tell he'd been away from civilization awhile—his hair flopped over one eyebrow and curled over the collar of his flannel shirt. Jo became conscious of a deep thankfulness.

Steve and Lee's deaths had destroyed her belief that Dan's crack troop was invincible.

Even now the memory closed her throat. And they'd come so close to losing him, too. But now she would never have to worry for him again. Never have to dread the daily news feeds. She forgave him for making their private joke so public.

Anton gesticulated to make a point and a beer bottle toppled off the counter. Dan caught it, looked up and smiled at her with all the old lazy affection. Of course he'd known she was there. Even in the dimly lit bar, his eyes were piercing.

"Here comes my bride."

"Great joke." She stepped into his hug. "Really hilarious."

His arms tightened. "I told you I'd find you a husband."

Jo pulled back.

Dan's eyes gleamed. "Miss me?"

"No." She broke free only to be pulled into Anton's embrace.

"Congratulations, Jo. Sheesh, you're a dark horse. Why the hell didn't you tell your old gang?"

"Because it's a joke."

Dan pulled a beer mat out of his jean pocket and handed it to Anton. "I have a contract."

"Give me that!"

Fending her off, Anton read it with a grin, then returned it to Dan. "Looks legal to me."

"If it makes you feel better, Swannie—" Dan repocketed it "—I'd warmed to the idea anyway."

"Gee, thanks." Jo relaxed. "What are you doing here?"

"Paying the deposit for the wedding breakfast."

"You always did like to labor a joke, Jansen. You know I mean in New Zealand. Why didn't you tell me you were coming home today?"

"I wanted the element of surprise." Under gold-tipped lashes, eyes as blue as the Mediterranean sparkled. Oh, yes, she'd missed him. "You know, Jo, it's kinda humiliating that you're the only one not taking me seriously here. I've already had a dozen RSVPs. Speaking of which…" He held out his hand to someone behind her. "Grant, hey, buddy. And Chris. Long time no see."

Jo shifted uneasily as the men exchanged handshakes. She wanted Dan to concede the joke, just not right now.

"You guys here on business?" Dan looked at Grant.

"We hope so." Chris had always liked to answer for other people. "You back farming now?"

"Trial run…could be permanent. Depends on whether Jo shows up for the wedding."

Jo forced a laugh. "Always a kidder." She put a hand under Chris's elbow. "Let's go back to our table. I know you movers and shakers work on a tight schedule."

Chris resisted. "I have to say I'm surprised, Dan. I never knew you were interested in Jo romantically."

"Obviously I had to wait for her to drop her standards," said Dan. "Let other guys disappoint her into having more realistic expectations. So I guess I have you to thank in some *small* way."

Jo caught Anton's eye, saw he was enjoying this as much as Dan. She bit her lip. At any other time she'd have loved having Chris put in his place but not when she was about to reject CommLink's offer. She wanted the atmosphere amicable. She flashed a quick frown at Dan, who interpreted it correctly.

"Still, I hear you're achieving great things in your career."

Some of the stiffness went out of Chris's posture. Jo realized she was still gripping his elbow and released it.

"Thanks. I hope your farming venture's as successful."

"You and me both. Anyway, I have an

appointment so I'd better get going. Jo…? I'll be at Barry's when you're done." The menswear shop downstairs from the *Chronicle*. His lips brushed hers and she blinked in surprise.

Dismissing a prickle of unease, Jo sat down with Chris and Grant over chicken pie. "About the paper."

"Always impatient," Chris said. "But before we present our offer let me tell you why it may be lower than you had hoped."

His comment intrigued her. Jo finished a morsel of creamy chicken and flaky golden pastry. "Go on."

"The situation's changed since you and I talked." Grant's tone was apologetic as he put down his fork and reached for his water glass. "The economic downturn's decimating revenue for all of us in community publishing."

"What my colleague's saying," Chris interrupted, "is that the *Chronicle*'s books showed a sharp drop for the six months ending in December."

"And a steady recovery this year," Jo pointed out.

"Not to anywhere near the previous year's levels," Chris countered.

Give me time. "How about we skip the preamble and go straight to your offer?"

"At least let's finish this delicious lunch first," he protested.

"Why, will the offer give me indigestion?"

Chris laughed, but when their plates had been cleared and he finally gave her the contract Jo did need an antacid to stomach it.

"You probably have questions," he said.

"Only one." Jo looked at Grant. "Did you have a hostile takeover in mind when you first approached me to sell?"

His mouth dropped open. "Of course not!" Out of the corner of her eye, Jo saw Chris shift in his chair.

"I believe you," she said to Grant. "You know, Chris, I sent you the *Chronicle*'s accounts in good faith. I guess I should have known that, sensing a weakness, you'd pounce."

"That's a little harsh." He seemed hurt as he picked up his dessert menu.

"Order the double chocolate cheesecake," Jo suggested. "It'll kill you quicker." She discovered she was enjoying herself.

Grant looked aghast, but Chris only laughed.

"To be honest I was feeling guilty when I came here today," she confessed. "You see, I'd already decided to decline your offer. How fortunate we've both been wasting each other's time."

The two men exchanged glances, then Grant leaned forward. "Jo, you've done a great job," he said earnestly. "In fact, you've held out longer than most small independents. But these days publishing success comes from economies of scale, not idealism."

Jo looked at Chris. "I'm assuming you're the bad cop."

"Always coming out swinging…well…okay." He put down the dessert menu. "Here are the facts. The *Chronicle*'s sixty-year monopoly in the region is no longer unassailable. The local population is more fluid—old loyalties hold less sway. It would be easy for us to set ourselves up in opposition and add value for advertisers."

"Yes, I've seen the puff pieces masquerading as impartial journalism in your publications. The *Chronicle* reflects the community's interests, not advertisers' interests."

Chris laughed. "Reports on every two-bit community group hardly make riveting reading, however inflammatory your news pages may be."

Grant shifted uncomfortably. "We've no wish to see an iconic brand fail. Neither do you, Jo, or you wouldn't have looked for a buyer. Obviously we'd prefer to negotiate a sale—one that works for both of us—rather than launch a competitive paper and slug it out in the market."

"But make no mistake," Chris smiled, "we will do just that if you turn us down."

Yes, she was definitely enjoying herself. "Give me your best offer," she said, "and I'll consider it."

When they'd left, she went to the bar, ordered a double espresso and nursed it in front of the fire. Chris had used Grant like a Trojan horse when Jo had been too beleaguered to smell a rat. The entrepreneur in her could appreciate his cleverness.

She slipped off the high heels she'd worn for this meeting and stretched her stockinged feet toward the fire. She was really going to enjoy teaching him a lesson. *I'm back.*

"Jo?"

Anton tapped her shoulder. His signet ring glinted in the firelight as he held out a piece of paper. "Dan forgot his receipt. Will you give it to him?"

Automatically she accepted it, then saw it was for a thousand-dollar deposit on a wedding supper. "Joke's getting kinda thin, Anton." Jo ripped it in two and dropped it on the coffee table.

His brow creased. "I thought the joke was in the way you proposed?"

She threw up her hands. "Why does everyone assume it's true?"

Anton picked up the pieces and handed them back. "Because jokers don't usually pay in cash."

CHAPTER FOUR

DAN KNEW JO HAD REALIZED he wasn't playing games as soon as he saw her striding down Main Street.

Through the plate-glass storefront she looked like a gunfighter at the O.K. Corral, purposeful, with a determined set to her delicate chin as she steeled herself to shoot down the buddy who'd gone loco.

Knowing her so well, he could even see she was a little frightened that he was so willfully destroying the status quo.

"Earth to Daniel, can we concentrate please?" He returned his attention to Barry, who was rifling through the racks of suits labeled Special Occasions. "I'm hearing a no to the cummerbund and bow tie?"

"You know me, Baz. A man of simple tastes." *Except in women.* "You choose."

Dan turned back to the window. Jo stood at the traffic lights, arms folded, foot tapping impatiently as she waited for the green.

The last time he'd seen her—at Auckland

Hospital after the funerals—she'd been recovering from surgery on a rotator cuff injury after a fall on her shoulder. Even shattered by grief Dan had seen she wasn't well enough to hear what he was going through so he'd said he was coping.

Barry's exasperated voice broke into his reverie. "Daniel Jansen, I've said the same thing three times." His friend planted his hands on his slim hips. "Black or charcoal gray for the stroller coat?"

"Charcoal gray." Outside Jo had been waylaid by a well-wisher. He watched her gesticulate, shaking her head. He smiled. "The color of the bride's eyes when she's pissed."

"We need a contrasting color for the waistcoat and tie." Barry flicked through the racks. "Taupe is hot this season."

Dan was momentarily diverted. "What the hell color is taupe?"

"Fawn." Barry pulled out a waistcoat to show him. "Is the bride going to be in white or ivory? You don't want clashes on the day."

"I think the clashes might be earlier than that." The anemic sun caught her short auburn curls. The new-look short hairstyle feathered around her cheekbones. It suited her.

"So the waistcoat…full back or backless?"

"Full back sounds more manly."

Barry grinned. "Not secure in your masculinity, sweetie?"

"Not with my bride bearing down on us. Hide the scissors."

The bell above the door jangled and Jo swept in. "What the hell is going on?" she demanded.

"We were discussing taupe," he said mildly.

Barry glanced from one to the other. "He wasn't supposed to come without you, was he? The naughty boy. Jo, I like your suit."

"Thanks." She took in the row of tuxedos and narrowed her gaze on Dan. "This farce has gone far enough."

"Now, why can't you just be swept away by the romance of it all?" Dan complained. "Baz, forget taupe. Give me a waistcoat in silver."

Jo grabbed the garment first. "Oh, yeah, very romantic. Organizing a wedding without the consent of the bride." Dan started to reach in his jean pocket. "And if you bring out the damn beer mat again, Jansen, I'll ram it down your throat." She handed the silver waistcoat back to Barry. "Of course he's not serious."

Dan raised his brows. "Why aren't I?"

"I don't even know why we're having this conversation." Exasperated, she turned on him. "For one, I'm not interested in marriage and kids anymore. With anyone. For two, you never were."

"Groom's prerogative to change his mind." Dan reached past her for the waistcoat. "But not the bride's."

Jo caught his hand in a death grip. "I'm trying to be diplomatic here."

He laughed. So did Barry.

"I'm making a list of aiders and abettors," she warned and Barry looked to him for guidance. Dan freed his hand from Jo's and gestured for the waistcoat.

Barry dithered. "You're both my friends.... I don't know whose side to take."

"Mine," Jo ordered.

Dan crooked one finger. Barry gave him the garment. "Sorry, Jo, he's brawn. You're mainly bluster. And, sweetie, he really does want to marry you."

"Why are you doing this?" Bewildered, she turned back to him.

Walking over to the mirror, Dan held the waistcoat against his chest. "You want a family—I'm ready to settle down. Who better to marry than the only woman I've ever had a halfway decent relationship with? It's a win-win for both of us."

She gave a strangled laugh. "Marriage isn't a business deal. There's a little matter of love."

"We love each other."

"Platonically!"

"That means it will last."

"For God's sake, Dan, get real. We've had fifteen years of being grown-ups when we could have got together and we never have. Doesn't that tell you something?"

"Yeah, that timing is everything." He smiled at her. "Hit on me again now."

A rare blush colored her cheeks. "We don't talk about that."

"We haven't talked about it." Dan shrugged on the waistcoat. "That doesn't mean either of us forgot. Baz, you look like a man in need of a coffee. Give us five minutes, will you?"

He waited until their buddy left the shop then said, "Funny, isn't it? At the time I was outraged that my best friend was coming on to me. But I never could get that image out of my head." His voice grew husky. "The way your breasts looked under that chiffony thing—"

"Don't!" She turned away and all he could see was her profile as she began spacing a row of jackets. "Don't build a future on one drunken pass I barely remember."

He did up the buttons on the waistcoat. "You suggested the marriage contract when you were drunk. You hit on me when you were drunk.

Maybe your subconscious was trying to tell you something."

She scoffed. "Yes, stop drinking cocktails. I don't get this sudden desire for matrimony. Didn't you say you'd never get married?"

"No, I said there was plenty of time." In the mirror some idiot was standing in jeans, a flannel shirt and a shiny silver-gray waistcoat.

There was a pregnant silence. "And you learned otherwise," she said in a low voice.

"Yeah, I learned otherwise." Dan unbuttoned and took off the vest, his fingers leaving faint traces of cold sweat on the satin back.

As a soldier he'd accepted his mortality. But his mates' deaths had rammed the lesson home on an emotional level that was hard to bear. "I can't bring Steve and Lee back but I can honor their memory by making sure I live big for all of us." *Live like it matters.* "Quit flitting from woman to woman and make my life count... settle down." He tossed the waistcoat aside, tried on another one in black. "Jeez, a moustache and I'd look like Wyatt Earp in this thing."

Shrugging it off, he reached for a coathanger and replaced it on the rack. "When I packed up my stuff and found that beer mat I got to thinking, it's not a stupid idea, marrying your best friend. You already know each other's faults. And all the boring bits are taken care of." He grinned. "Respect, commitment, loyalty. Which leaves the fun stuff to work on, like hot sex."

He looked over at her, his smile fading. "Given a do-over, Jo, I wouldn't turn you down again."

"But you don't get a do-over." Her face was pale, her gaze steady. "You said I'd be relieved you rejected me when I sobered up, and you were right." She took a deep breath. "I'm sorry about the tragedy overseas, but I want to leave our friendship as it is. And as I've already said, I don't want a family anymore."

He watched the pulse beating fast in her throat. "I don't believe you."

"It doesn't matter. I'm not marrying you."

Dan picked up the silver waistcoat and rehung it. "You need some time to get used to the idea," he said. "Here's the deal. I'll organize the wedding, all you have to do is decide whether to show up."

"Of course I'm not going to show up!"

"See, that's one of your faults—snap judgments," he said kindly. "Try and keep an open mind. My failing, as you know, is stubbornness. Which sets us up for one hell of an interesting few weeks, doesn't it?"

As she stared at him, speechless, Barry stuck his head around the door. He took silence as safety and came in, holding a take-out coffee.

"All sorted?"

"Nearly," said Dan. "So, honey, you weren't serious about our bridesmaids wearing pink, were you?"

"Pink!" Barry threw up his hands. "Jo, with your red hair?"

His bride finally found her voice. "I am *not* marrying you!" Cheeks flushed, she advanced on him. "Quit fooling around and tell Baz."

"Uh-huh." Dan put on a top hat, tilting it as he checked his reflection. "I'm practicing being a husband…soothing noises, not really listening."

Jo knocked his top hat off, and with a squawk, Barry scrambled to rescue it.

"You seriously want to play chicken?" she asked incredulously. "With *me?*"

"I was thinking tonight we could start working on the fun stuff."

She turned on her heel and wrenched open the door. *Dingalingaling.*

He went to the doorway, waiting until she was fifty yards down the road. "If you really weren't interested you wouldn't have jumped me in Auckland!" he called.

Glancing at interested passersby, she hurried back to hiss. "I was *drunk!*"

"Like I said then, the only time I've seen you drunk like that is when you're in trouble."

She looked away. "That's ridiculous."

"We became mates when we were five years old because you'd decided I'd be useful for carrying things. I'm still good at sharing the load, Jo."

She held his gaze. "Help me. My best friend's crazy."

Dan leaned against the doorjamb. "How did your business meeting go?"

Jo blinked. "Couldn't be better."

"I hear Nan's been diagnosed with dementia."

Jo lost her composure. "I wish people would mind their damn business."

"I'll tell Mom that."

Her expression became hopeful. "She *can't* approve of this."

"See how much you've already got in common?"

"Ahhh!" She walked away, came back. "Dan, you're my escape buddy, don't do this to us."

"Did you ever see that Costner movie, *Field of Dreams?* About the guy who built a baseball field in a cornfield? It didn't make sense even to him. He only knew he had to do it."

"That's the dumbest reason I ever heard."

Barry joined him at the door and they watched Jo's retreating figure. "What was that about?"

"Bridal nerves."

"It didn't actually sound like she wanted to marry you, Dan," he ventured.

"No," he admitted. "But I've got twenty-two days to change her mind."

"So you have a Plan B, then?"

Dan snorted. "Mate, I expect to hit the end of the alphabet before the wedding day."

JO SWEPT ALONG MAIN Street resisting the urge to barrel through pedestrians coming the other way.

Typical of Dan to think he could stroll in and change the rules on a whim.

Oncoming pedestrians started giving her a wider berth but, her eyes fixed on the pavement and her fists clenched, Jo barely noticed. All she'd suggested was one roll in the hay and he couldn't even do her that favor. Now he was adding insult to injury by telling her she was the One…he'd settle for. And expecting her to settle, too. Her high heels wobbled, forcing her to slow down.

Admittedly she'd let him think her desperate seduction had been driven by her fear of ending up alone and childless, but, dammit, her best friend should know her better than that. She was not—and never would be—pathetic and needy! Which was precisely why she hadn't told him the truth. Actually this would be funny if it wasn't so *bloody* infuriating.

A horn tooted. The jeweler waved from his Volvo, stopped at the lights. "Congratulations, Jo," he called through the open window. "Dan's a great guy."

"No, he's not and we're—" the light changed and the car pulled away. She jogged two or three steps in chase before the heels stopped her "—*not* getting married!"

The girly *tap, tap, tap* of her shoes exacerbated her anger. *To hell with this.* Jo stepped out of them, feeling the chill pavement through her stockings. Someone bumped into her from behind.

Mrs. Beasley, a crony of Nan's, adjusted her hat. "My dear, I've been calling out to you for ages. I hear from the butcher that—"

"We are *not* getting married!"

"It's your birthday," Mrs. B finished in confusion. "Are you…having a happy day?"

"Thanks, Mrs. B. Yes." Jo smiled through clenched teeth. The old lady's gaze shifted to the shoes Jo held in her hand.

Jo said nothing and Mrs. B lost her nerve. "Where are you off to in such a hurry?"

"I'm…" Jo trailed off. In her rage she'd walked halfway down the street instead of going upstairs to the *Chronicle*. "Well, nice to see you. Goodbye." Jo started striding back in the direction she'd come.

"Who aren't you marrying?" Mrs. B called hopefully. "I can tell people."

Great. The biggest gossip in Beacon Bay on the case.

Somehow she had to fix this. Her steps slowed, Jo realized, because she was almost at the menswear store again. *Dammit, I am not changing how I treat my best friend.*

Dropping her heels onto the pavement, she stepped into them and straightened her suit jacket with a short, sharp jerk. Then with every muscle twitching to run, Jo strolled past the plate glass storefront. *I will not look, I will not so much as glance in that window. I am unconcerned.*

Her gaze darted left and two images were burned in her brain. Her reflected face, eyes furtive, hunted. And her would-be groom, naked to the waist, lean muscle rippling as he shrugged on a starched white shirt.

She was past. Jo tugged open the *Chronicle*'s door and took the stairs two at a time. Halfway up she stopped and leaned her forehead against the wall. "Why are you doing this to us *now?*" she whispered. And going public was tantamount to emotional blackmail. Jo continued up the stairs.

The newsroom was empty. Tomorrow's paper was done—Jo only had to sign off on it before delivering it to the printers—but still, 4:00 p.m. was early to close an issue. In her office, she dumped her bag on her desk then sank into her chair and leaned forward over the desk, head on her arms. *Loser's posture.* She sat up straight again, staring sightlessly at the screen.

She should be strategizing. Instead all she could think about was Dan's extraordinary behavior. Maybe she was overreacting—maybe he was simply pushing the joke to its absolute limit and everyone was in on it? Any minute now he'd appear with a grin and a gotcha. Yes, that was it. Of course it was. She relaxed in her chair. There was no other rational explanation.

The phone rang. That was probably him now. "You got me—"

"It's Delwyn. I think I left my invoice book in the staff room. Can you check for me?"

"Sure." Jo walked to the staff room and opened the door. Glimpsing red balloons imprinted with *Happy Birthday,* she closed it again.

The door burst open and her beaming staff threw their arms high. "Surprise!"

"WHERE'S MY INVITE? I had the housekeeper check the mailbox twice."

Jo's grip tightened on the phone, her delight at the birthday call dissipating.

"You're on a yacht in Vava'u—how the hell do you know about this?" Maybe her second-best friend wasn't on a family holiday in Tonga for six weeks. Maybe—

"Luke was reading the *Herald* online and saw it in the notices."

"Hang on a minute." Jo pulled up New Zealand's largest daily newspaper on the internet. "'Daniel Jansen is delighted to announce his engagement to Jocelyn Swann.' I'll kill him." She was starting to mean it.

"So you're not getting married?"

As she brought the former mayor of Beacon Bay up to speed, Jo's cell rang. Caller ID showed it was Nan. "Liz, I've gotta go, love to Luke… Hi, Nan, how lovely to talk to you."

"Darling, did I forget that you're getting married?"

Jo rubbed her throbbing temples. "No, love, ignore the invitation. It's one of Dan's jokes."

"Such a nice boy, Daniel."

"That's one word for him."

"My wedding dress might fit you with a little adjustment I think." A former dressmaker, Nan had always been stylish, matching gloves, bag and shoes. Jo recalled this morning's mismatch

of gardening hat and dressing gown with a pang
of regret.

"Except it's a joke, Nan," she reminded her
patiently.

"Such a nice boy, Daniel."

It was hopeless to persist when Rosemary was
in one of her loops. And it didn't matter because
in ten minutes she'd have forgotten. But other
people wouldn't. "I'll see you tomorrow. Tell
Polly I'll explain later." Jo hung up and hauled
the production manager out of the staff room
where he was enjoying his third beer and made
him design a last-minute ad for tomorrow's edition. Bold font. Big type. Dan would know there
was no room for confusion on this, no room for
hope. Or doubt.

"Jo Swann and Dan Jansen are not getting
married. It was a joke, people!" A smiley emoticon should take the sting out of it.

Because it was so funny.

By the time Jo had deflected Kevin with
an "I promise we'll discuss the CommLink
meeting tomorrow," and made it home from
her impromptu birthday celebration, she had a
throbbing headache.

Conscious of Polly's threat to check for
lights on too early she left the curtains open
and navigated the stairs by moonlight. A lanky
shadow on the landing made her gasp until she

recognized the lampstand from the living room. Nan had been moving things again. Pushing it to one side—she was too tired to tidy up now—Jo went into her bedroom, stripped off her clothes, put on her dressing gown, then ran a bath. While it filled she sat on the rim and listening to the house creaking and groaning as the outside temperature dropped. Steam rose, invisible in the dark. It touched Jo's face with warm, sympathetic tendrils.

The doorbell rang, startling her. Wiping her eyes, she groped for the tap and turned it off. The bell rang again, a peal that echoed through the dark, silent house. Jo didn't move. Silence except for the steady drip of the tap. Finally, she heard footsteps retreating down the gravel path. Clutching her robe, she crept to her bedroom window, which provided a view of the front garden.

Holding a bunch of white lilies, Dan stood under a bright moon. She froze but he'd caught her movement and lifted his face. Across the garden they stared at each other.

He'd changed into a white shirt and his broad shoulders were accentuated under the moon, which also bladed his cheekbones and shadowed his deep-set eyes. But Jo read his lips.

"Let me in."

Her heart started pumping so hard she struggled to breathe. She shook her head.

Dan assessed a route. She could read his thoughts. Swing up onto the pergola; walk along it to her window. Jo caught the sill for support as his gaze returned to hers, unblinking. Intent.

"No!" Through her panic, she found the fierceness she needed. The anger that her best friend was putting them through this when she was finally bringing some control back to her life.

Jerking the drapes together, she fumbled for the catch on the window and locked it. Counted one minute down, then two. Sucking in a fortifying breath she peeked again, half expecting to see Dan crouched on her windowsill. But there were only lilies propped against the gate. Bridal white in the moonlight.

Closing the drapes, Jo hugged herself as she returned to the bathroom and switched on the light. In the mirror her eyes were huge... shocked. He was really serious about this? Maybe she should tell him the truth behind that pass...

"Do you want his pity?"

No. God, no. Unthinkable. She hadn't protected her secret so carefully to reveal it now. She'd only panicked because she'd been caught unprepared.

Untying her robe, Jo shrugged it off her shoulders. Her gaze lowered over her naked body, then she turned and stepped into the hot, steamy water, leaned back and closed her eyes.

In company with the real Jo, his best friend, he'd soon come to his senses. He had to.

CHAPTER FIVE

A HAWK SWOOPED OVER the pasture, its silhouette faint against the grass in the dawn light. Dan turned off the hurricane lamp he'd been using to illuminate his fencing work and stretched his back, his gaze following the predator as it crested a hill with one lazy flap then disappeared into the rising sun.

He returned his attention to tightening the wire with the strainer then tied it off and surveyed the seven-wire fence. All he had to do was add wooden battens for bracing and this stretch was done. Straightening his back, he took a break.

Amazing what insomnia could achieve. For the past two nights he'd risen around four and gone fencing, rigging up lighting to help him do it.

Fortunately there was more than enough maintenance work to absorb his restless energy.

The sky lightened to lavender-blue. It was going to be a beautiful morning. On impulse he started up the hill for a better view of the sunrise, attracting the attention of the steers in the next paddock, which trotted over to the fence. They were yearlings, curious and still skittish. One spooked and bolted and the rest thundered along behind, stopping in confusion three hundred meters away, their breath steaming clouds in the growing light.

Untying the woolen bush jacket from his waist, Dan pulled it on as he climbed, tempted to use his cell to call Jo. *Come watch the sunrise with me.* Except that would only confirm his craziness in her eyes. He thought of her fury the other night, when he'd gone visiting with flowers in the moonlight. Better give her one more day to cool off.

A breeze came up, carrying the malodorous stench of semi-rotted grass. Silage. Dan grinned. Not such a romantic setting after all. Reaching the crest, he stripped off his sweaty fencing gloves as the sunrise slowly illuminated the rolling pasture. Sheep dotted the steeper sections while mobs of bulls—small groups of thirty animals—populated the flat, separated by electric fences.

It had rained overnight, swelling the stream which now ran muddy and fast through the property. He traced it back to its source, a spring-formed lake surrounded by marshland and bog, thick with reeds and waterfowl. Duck-shooting season started this weekend, he thought. Mist rose in patches off the dew-soaked grass, spiraling lazily toward the sun.

How many times had he imagined this view in the harsh, throat-scratching desert? This stillness. Dan closed his eyes. But even with his ears attuned to the minutiae of country noises—the soft snort of cattle, the birdsong, the faint throb of a tractor engine—peace eluded him.

I should have been there.

He opened his eyes, simultaneously closing his mind to the images that haunted him. Below, his father was a tiny figure on the tractor as he hauled silage into the northwest paddock, half a dozen working dogs running behind him. That was another job ahead. Getting the dogs to change loyalties. Giving up on serenity, Dan returned to stapling fence battens.

Herman might be sleeping in town but his waking hours were all on the farm. To help Dan while the farmhand was on holiday, he told Pat when she tried to finalize travel itineraries. To free you up to organize the wedding, he'd tell his son. But for all his talk of a succession plan, his father seemed reluctant to implement one. Still, Dan preferred Herman's company to being alone. What if Jo didn't come around?

He rammed the batten in place. No, defeat wasn't an option. Dan lost himself in physical labor. When he'd finished the sun was high and his stomach rumbled. Returning to the ATV— the quad bike that handled the farm's varied terrain—he saw a curl of smoke rising from the direction of the homestead.

Only Mom would light the fire during the day, Herman being too economical and Dan too inured to climate to bother. The quad rattled over the main track and he made a mental note to discuss regrading with his father.

Go faster, Danny. Steve's voice came to him, vibrating with a child's excitement. C'mon, chicken. *Uncle Herman doesn't need to know.* His older cousin could always tease him into being recklesss. *Let's see if we can get some air on this thing.*

Dan smiled in the chill morning. Oh, yeah, they got air all right. Only luck had saved them from being hurt. But nothing had saved them from Herman's wrath when he saw the damage to the ATV. They'd spent a week cutting wood for that one.

His vision blurred. He blinked hard.

Two of the five of them dead and, eleven months later, two survivors still in bad shape. Ross was rehabilitating from horrific injuries; Nate had left the service and was roaming the States.

A tooth abscess had saved Dan from the

ambush. He'd been at the dentist when the news
came through. His gum numb with novocaine,
he'd run to join the retrieval team. The pain of
a half-drilled tooth kicked in as the anesthetic
wore off but he'd welcomed it. Blazing twisted
scraps were all that remained of the vehicle. Of
Steve.

Lee had been missing and Nate crouched
behind meager cover, holding off the enemy
with Ross bloody and unconscious at his feet.
Later, Dan had to peel a dazed Nate's fingers
from his weapon. He'd seen that look before,
knew what it meant. Some experiences took a
man past a point he couldn't go…because if he
did, he couldn't serve.

His knuckles whitened on the ATV's handles.

Lee had been found the next day…what was
left of him. His body had been packed with
explosives and detonated in the desert. Un-
identifiable except by eyewitness accounts and
an engagement ring he'd intended to give his
girlfriend on his return.

I should have been there.

Maybe he could have done something…
changed something. Though everyone and
logic told him otherwise he couldn't shake these
pointless, debilitating thoughts that still shadowed him like buzzards.

Dan had always been robust, whether through

a gift of genes or an inborn balance. Whatever it was, psychological tests said he had it. The ability to endure. With an effort, he loosened his grip on the handles, dropped the throttle. The only way through this was holding on to the person who always grounded him.

Everything came back to Jo.

HIS MOM'S NISSAN WAS parked by the farmhouse, a mattress on the roof rack. Dan had asked to borrow one until he could go shopping for furniture with Jo.

"Always the optimist, Danny," Steve used to say to him.

"Damn right."

He'd refused to sleep even one night on the lumpy double bed his dad had been using. Drawing abreast of the car he saw the mattress was a single and laughed. Well, if she thought a single mattress would stop her baby boy from having sex with his intended, assuming Dan could get Jo there, she was dreaming.

To hell with it. He'd make time to buy a king-size tomorrow.

He found Pat stuck in the doorway wrestling with an armchair as big as she was.

"What are you doing moving that on your own?"

"I can manage," she insisted, but massaged

her lower back after he took the chair off her. Small and slender with a swing of shoulder-length hair only lightly threaded with gray, Pat Jansen bore a close resemblance to Diane Keaton. "I only brought one comfortable chair," she added, "so make sure you get it."

Dan maneuvered the wide-bodied chair through the doorway. "Okay, we're alone. Tell me what's going on with you and Dad?" There had always been stressful undercurrents in his parents' marriage but they seemed to have turned into whitewater, at least on Mom's part. Like his son, Herman kept his troubles to himself.

She caught a falling cushion as he plonked the chair next to the fireplace. "Nothing." She'd cleaned the house. Lemon polish scented the air and there weren't as many dust motes in the sunlight streaming through the window. "At least nothing for you to worry about." A small coffee table sat like an island in the middle of the empty room. The dog slunk out from under it, looking guilty for being caught inside.

"It's okay, boy." Dan fondled his ears. "You're retired now, too, remember?"

He knew Pat was waiting for a follow-up question. It was always this way with Mom. You had to work to find out what was wrong. Except playing chicken with his resistant bride would require nerves of steel. He couldn't afford to get embroiled in his parents' marital issues. Anyway, empathy was a girl thing; better Mom phoned one of the twins—Merry in Auckland or Viv in New York. On second thought, not Viv.

Pat gave up waiting and surveyed the sparsely furnished room. "We've got to make this place welcoming enough for you to stay. I'll bring the spare couch next visit."

"Of course I'm staying. I'm getting married, remember?"

"Honey, I have bad news." If it was bad, why did she sound so relieved? "Come look at this." In the kitchen, Pat pointed to a quarter-page ad in the *Chronicle*. "Jo Swann and Dan Jansen are not getting married. It was a joke, people! ☺"

Dan grinned at the smilie emoticon.

"You're taking this very well," his mother said uneasily. She knew that grin.

He took out his cell, checking the paper's index for the direct line to sales.

"Hi…Delwyn, it's Dan. Yeah, well, don't be sorry. No, my feelings aren't hurt. Listen, how much is an ad in your paper, same size?" As he told the rep what he wanted, his mother started unpacking the cutlery from a cardboard box on the kitchen counter. Dan had to raise his voice above the clatter to finish the call. "I'm happy to pay a premium for the front page... See you later, then."

When he'd rung off, he leaned against the counter top. "Okay, Mom, spit it out. Why don't you approve?"

His mother had always been ambivalent about Jo, often reading his friend's assertiveness as aggression and her frankness as rudeness. She didn't understand that her son found these qualities refreshing precisely because he'd been brought up by Jo's opposite.

Tight-lipped martyrdom and "guess what I'm feeling"—these were things to cower men, not a woman comfortable asking for what she wanted.

"It's not about whether *I* approve." Opening the oven, Pat pulled out a bacon-and-egg pie. On the bottom shelf Dan saw a batch of rising scones. "Though I think your approach is all wrong."

"There's method in my madness."

Pat frowned.

Damn, wrong word. She already had doubts about his mental health.

"She can be so...forceful, Danny. I'm worried she'll try and run your life."

Dan hid a smile. Talk about the pot calling the kettle black. His mom had wanted him to be a lawyer, something civilized. But Jo had always understood his need to test himself. Like he understood hers. And unlike every other female in his life, his best friend never asked for more than he was prepared to give. "I've made up my mind, Mom."

"Fine, let's change the subject." Sighing, Pat began slicing the pie. "I talked to Ellie this morning." Steve's mother.

Turning away, Dan plugged in the kettle.

"She's hoping you'll find time to visit when you've settled in." Steve's parents lived an hour south.

Herman understood no-go zones but his mother was a different story. "It's on my list."

"They're all worried about Lewis," she persisted.

His godson? Dan looked over. "What's wrong with him?"

"He's getting stomachaches…off school a lot. The doctor can't find anything wrong with him. Says it's growing pains."

His own gut knotted, as it always did thinking about his cousin's widow, Claire, and their son. She'd insisted there was nothing he could do for her and turned down money when Dan, Ross and Nate offered it. "He is thirteen."

"Ellie says he's withdrawn and only wants to sit on the PlayStation all day."

That wasn't the kid Dan remembered. The kid who wanted to be outside doing boy stuff with his dad. He said gruffly, "He lost his father this year, Mom. It's going to take time to adjust."

"Well, have you phoned Claire lately?" Taking some mugs off the draining board, Dan considered his reply. Since the funeral, he'd made a point of calling Claire every month. But the conversations were stilted. Both of them pretending to be doing better than they were. Lately, he'd spun the calls out to every six weeks.

"I'm about due," he admitted. The kettle boiled and switched off. His mother pulled a silver teapot out of one of the boxes in the kitchen. He felt himself suddenly suffocating. "Mom, I don't need all this stuff."

"Teabags in mugs is for camping."

Dan wished he were back in the wilderness. "Sit down," he said. "Let me wait on you for a change." He parked her in a chair, then finished making the tea, plating up pie and buttering scones. He'd missed her cooking, if not her concern.

"And you haven't sent Steve's parents or Claire invitations to your wedding. That must mean you're not sure about marrying Jo."

That wasn't the reason, but Dan wasn't prepared to discuss it. He gave in to the inevitable. "I'll post them tomorrow."

Pat cleared her throat. "Danny, did you see anyone…afterward? A psychologist or grief counselor…"

"It's sorted." The SAS looked after its own.

"Are you sleeping yet?"

"Enough." The second night he'd stayed in his parents' new house. A mistake. Mom had caught him pacing at two in the morning. Only later did he wonder what caused *her* insomnia.

"Danny, I'm worried about you."

He flashed her a smile, a good one. "You like worrying, Mom."

"I brought some books with me that might be helpful."

Oh, God. He didn't need to look at the collection she dragged out of her bag to know the titles would contain words like *healing, inner child* and *transformational.* She devoured self-help manuals, chiefly for inspiration on how to change his father.

"Thanks." A glance out the window gave him an escape route. "Looks like some showers are coming. I'll go get the bed off the roof-rack." He paused at the doorway. "How did you get it up there?"

"A neighbor helped. Of course it would have been easier if your father was around," she added tartly. "Dan, please don't encourage Herman to think he's got all the time in the world to do this changeover. It's time your father made good on his word."

He touched hand to heart. "I promise to stay a *neutral* party."

His mother didn't take the hint. "I mean, is it so bad traveling Europe for three months and spending quality time with your wife?"

Dan tried again. "Talk to Herman, Mom."

"You think I haven't?" she snapped, then collected herself and gave him a tremulous smile. "No, you're right. It's not fair to make you take sides."

Sides? Alarmed, Dan headed for the door. "I'll get that bed."

AT ELEVEN THURSDAY MORNING a courier delivered CommLink's final offer. Kevin raced into her office with it, closing the door and pulling the blinds like a conspirator. Jo wished she hadn't told him. He was taking it all so seriously, even though she'd assured him she could handle it.

The poor guy had had his faith in her shaken over the past year. "Think of it as a team-building exercise," she'd told him. "Close your eyes, fall back and I'll catch you."

He wasn't amused. "This is no time for jokes. I've been researching CommLink over the last couple of days. They've got a history of picking up financially distressed companies—"

"We're not distressed, merely uncomfortable."

"And setting up competitive newspapers."

Perusing the contract, Jo didn't answer. "What do you know," she said, "it's actually fair. Grant must have squeezed Chris. Offer expires on May 18."

"That's only two weeks. We've got no time to rebuild advertising for a prolonged siege."

"Relax. It will take them months to set up a paper—if they're serious."

"I made a few calls. They can set up within weeks of a final no."

"I made a few calls, too. They've been sitting on their hands for eighteen months. And Grant implied the economic downturn has affected them as much as us."

Kev looked hopeful. "You think they're bluffing."

"My instincts are pretty good about these things."

He looked at her oddly.

"What?"

"Didn't you say that about Dan?" This morning's edition of the *Chronicle* lay unread on her desk. Kevin unfolded it and laid it flat. Jo's eyes settled on the strip ad along the bottom of the front page. And widened.

Bridal nerves have settled. Wedding back on. ☺

For a moment she gawked at it, then pushed to her feet and headed to the sales department. "Who accepted this?"

Delwyn's gaze darted to the paper clenched in Jo's fist, then around the room like a panicked swallow fluttering for an exit. Bingo. Jo dropped the paper on the sales rep's desk.

"He paid the most expensive rate. And you told us to take anything in the current economy." Seeing Jo wasn't buying it, Delwyn whimpered. "Okay, I'm a sucker for romance."

"This isn't romance, it's a declaration of war. And you're on *my* side." Her voice rose. "Hear that, people? *My* side. The only advertisement you accept from Dan Jansen is a retraction. Am. I. Clear?" Heads nodded vigorously. "Once and for all—we are not getting married."

Delwyn waved for Jo's attention. "Does that mean not helping him outside work, too?"

Her headache started coming back. "What do you mean?"

"We met for coffee yesterday and I gave him details of the florist, baker and photographer I'm using for my wedding." Delwyn waved a sheet of pink notepaper. "He was doing the rounds this morning."

"Is that the list?" Jo snatched it away from her. "I'm on my cell if anyone needs me."

At the baker's she learned that Dan was torn between angel food cake and traditional fruitcake; at the florist's that he couldn't decide between white roses and ivy or red roses and baby's breath. The photographer said she'd just missed her fiancé, but she'd catch him at Baxter's Department Store. "He's setting up a gift registry."

She hoped Dan wasn't anywhere near blenders, knives or glassware. She finally tracked him down in the furniture section where he was testing a king-size bed.

"Great timing," he approved. "I need a second opinion. I'm thinking too bouncy."

Jo picked up a pillow and hurled it at him. "Quit making a spectacle of us."

Catching it, Dan propped the pillow behind his head. "I wasn't the one who took our private life into print."

"My ad was designed to save you further humiliation by making a joke of it, but it seems you're determined to suffer."

"If I'm going to be left, it has to be at the altar." He rolled off the bed. "So, Grant tells me CommLink made an offer for the *Chronicle*."

Jo felt her jaw drop. "What were you doing with Grant?"

"Having a quiet drink with an old school friend. If my bride won't spend time with me, I've got to hang out with someone."

"I can't believe Grant breached confidentiality."

"Well, he was pretty hammered at the time," Dan confided. "You know he can't hold his liquor."

She narrowed her eyes. "You got him drunk."

"If you won't tell me what's going on, what choice did I have?" he said reasonably.

"What else did he say?"

"That he hates his boss. Is it true, you invited an offer?"

"I was curious to know what the paper was worth."

"So you're not serious about selling?"

Jo shook her head. "Keep that quiet, though. I'm still working out the best way to say no." She added pointedly, "Some people aren't always good at listening."

Dan grinned, then lay down on another bed. "This one's got memory foam, which will apparently mould to our bodies."

"Your body," she corrected. "I have a bed."

"A single bed," he dismissed. "I'm talking

marital." He took all the legitimacy out of the word, made it wicked.

Jo put her hands on her hips. "Dan, I'm losing patience."

"*You're* losing patience?" She found herself lying on the mattress, his weight on top of her. "Are you really going to make me wait until the wedding night?"

Jo tried to wiggle free. "There isn't going to be a wedding night because there isn't going to be a wedding." Effortlessly Dan held her pinned and she gave up the undignified struggle and craned her neck to see where the sales assistant was. Engrossed on the phone, thank God. "What the hell's gotten into you?" she demanded. "The old Dan would never have done this."

"More fool him," he said and lowered his head to kiss her. Jo froze.

"You folks okay here?"

Pushing free, Jo scrambled off the bed and straightened her tailored shirt with the gathered bust.

On the bed, Dan put his hands behind his head. "We'll take it…unless there's one in a larger size? We like a big playground don't we, honey? And that leaves plenty of room for the kids."

Jo turned to the mirror and concentrated on raking a hand through her disheveled curls.

Sensing it wasn't in his best interests, the salesman didn't press her. "Let me go see if we have a super-king in the storeroom."

When he'd hurried away, she crossed to the bed and looked down at Dan.

"Is there *anything* I can say to make you stop this?"

He swung his feet to the floor. "Not a damn thing."

"Fine," she shoved him flat. "Play your games but play them solo. Order the cake and the flowers…I don't care. But I'm not seeing you again until you come to your senses."

Before she walked out, Jo noticed Dan no longer looked so smug. If you wanted to douse a fire, you took away the fuel. And he wasn't the only one capable of finding allies in the enemy camp. She should have thought of this earlier.

Jo took out her cell and dialed. "I know this is a surprise," she said after exchanging greetings, "but I think we need to talk."

CHAPTER SIX

"WHAT A LOVELY IDEA," Pat gushed as she embraced Jo at the garden-center café. "Meeting here to celebrate, just us two girls. You know I've been meaning to phone and congratulate you but it's all been so confusing. On, then off, then on again."

"Relax," said Jo. "I'm not marrying your son."

The older woman sank into an wrought-iron chair. "Thank God."

"Ouch." Jo took her own seat. "Maybe I do prefer it when you pretend to like me."

Pat recovered. "It's not that I don't like you... For heaven's sake, Jo, do you have to be so...so challenging all the time?"

"I'm sorry, I was brought up to be honest. From your reaction, I guess I'm not the only one wondering if Dan's sudden obsession with marrying me is a little odd."

The waitress arrived. "Can I take your order?"

"Cappuccino, skinny milk please, caffeine-free." Pat scanned the luscious cake selection in the cabinet behind them. "Nothing for me."

Jo admired self-control but Pat's bordered on self-flagellation. She reminded Jo of a Victorian missionary who persisted in wearing corsets in the tropics.

"Espresso and a piece of chocolate gâteau please." Jo glanced mischievously at Pat. "Two forks."

"One," Pat corrected. As usual they were off to a great start.

Jo stuck to what they had in common. "How has Dan acted since he got back?"

"Herman says half the work's done by the time he gets to the farm every morning, which means Danny's still not sleeping." Their order arrived as she told Jo about Dan's insomnia.

Absently, Pat sipped her cappuccino. "I wondered if it was some kind of post traumatic stress disorder, except, as Danny pointed out, he wasn't on patrol."

"But he was on the retrieval crew," said Jo slowly. She couldn't imagine what that had been like.

"And let's face it," said Pat, "he can't be in his right mind if he wants to—" She stopped, embarrassed.

Amusement pierced Jo's growing disquiet. "Marry me?"

"—proceed with this wedding against your wishes. Don't put words in my mouth."

"Sorry," Jo said meekly.

"All I'm saying is don't accept him if you have doubts. Marriage is hard work and you need one hundred percent commitment from the start. Even with commitment, there are no guarantees." She sounded disheartened. Jo proffered her a fork and, rolling the glazed cherry to the side of the plate, Pat dug into the chilled frosting.

"Well, you can relax about the marriage thing. I'm shunning Dan until he backs off."

She'd expected approval; instead Pat looked up horrified. "You can't do that, you're the only one he's likely to open up to. He's not talking to Herman about it and God knows," she added bitterly, "he refuses to confide in me."

Dismayed, Jo picked up her fork. "I hadn't thought of that." In silence, the two women shared the gâteau. When the last crumb had gone, Pat dabbed at her mouth to remove the evidence and gave Jo a pleading look.

"I wouldn't ask if I weren't worried sick about him…"

"Okay," Jo said, feeling trapped. "I won't shut him out completely."

A UTE SHE DIDN'T recognize was parked in the driveway when Jo got home in the deep twilight.

And the light was on in the parlor, the formal living room where Nan had once entertained her many visitors. Jo couldn't remember seeing anything in her grandmother's diary, but given the chaos of the past few days, she could have missed it.

In the garage, she turned off the headlights and sat for a moment in the dark. Then hauling her heavy briefcase from the passenger seat, she entered the house.

Perry Como crooned from the CD player and her mood lifted. Nan always played him when she was feeling well. Dumping her briefcase, she strolled into the parlor and stopped dead.

"Darling," said Nan. "We were just talking about you."

Dan filled another glass with champagne. "Tough day?"

"You could say that," she returned evenly, glaring at him. Accepting the glass, she turned to Nan, trying to recall how alcohol affected her medication. "Should you be drinking?"

"Pooh, one won't kill me." Her grandmother toasted Dan. "Besides, we're closing a deal."

Perry warbled that everyone knew where this was heading.

"What deal?"

"Daniel has offered to prune the hedges this weekend."

"He has enough to do on the farm." Despite her promise to Pat, Jo couldn't keep the sharpness out of her voice. He was boxing her in, closing off all escape routes.

Nan's smile faltered. "Oh, dear, why didn't I think of that?"

Dan leaned forward and chinked his glass to Rosemary's. "Because you know I'll always make time for my favorite women," he returned gallantly.

"Poppycock," Nan retorted, but she was smiling again. The three of them together was almost like old times. Almost. Jo sipped the champagne, holding the bubbles on her tongue before swallowing. Well, if the mountain thought coming to Mohammed would further its cause, the mountain thought wrong. "How about we go for a drive in the morning, Nan? Get out of Dan's way."

His eyes gleamed appreciatively.

Nan looked appalled. "You can't leave a man alone with a chainsaw, Jocelyn."

"Anyway, your part of the deal is to supply lunch," Dan said smoothly. He turned to Nan. "But if you feel I'm intruding…"

"Nonsense," protested Rosemary, "you're practically family."

Perry crooned about two hearts forever

linked. Jo gulped her champagne. "Where's Polly?" she asked her grandmother.

Dan answered. "The housekeeper? She's making dinner."

"Jocelyn, we've had such fun talking about when you two were children," said Rosemary. The more her grandmother lost of the present, the sharper the past seemed to become. "Tell me, Daniel, are you still intending to join the army?"

He looked puzzled, and Jo's fingers tightened on the stem of her glass.

"You mean *rejoin* the army?" he asked. "No, my resignation's permanent. And I'm back to take over the farm from Herman, remember?"

Nan sat back in the armchair and played with her pearls. "Oh, yes, of course." She sought out Jo, no longer a grande dame but a confused child.

"We like this tune," Jo reminded her as another old-timer, Vince Bugatti, began to croon. "You know I'll never leave you," she sang softly.

Nan's expression cleared. "No one cares like I do," she finished in a sweet contralto. "Vince Bugatti." Confidence restored, she turned back to Dan. "You grew up extremely handsome, Daniel. In fact, you have quite the look of my Graham, don't you think, Jocelyn?"

Instinctively Jo exchanged a smile with Dan. "I think Pops was a little rounder."

"And balder," said Dan.

"Not when I married him." Nan's brow furrowed. "Someone else is getting married soon."

Jo stiffened. "No, they're not."

"I'm sure they are." Her grandmother's voice was querulous again. She rummaged through her black handbag. "I write things down," she said to Dan. "Because of my memory… Jocelyn, what have you done with my notebook?" Her tone accusatory, Nan tipped the contents of her bag on the coffee table. Loose paper fluttered to the floor, along with four spoons, two potatoes and a dirty gardening trowel. "Have you been stealing from me?"

"Now, Nan," Jo cajoled, kneeling to collect the debris. "You know I'd never touch your notebook without permission."

Every night, she emptied the handbag of oddities Nan had squirreled away, but the notebook was sacrosanct.

"I don't believe you," Rosemary's voice rose hysterically. "I know you sneak into my—"

"Is this it?" Dan asked calmly. Coming forward, he slid a hand down the side of the chair, pulled out the notebook and placed it into Nan's shaking hands, then cupped them in reassurance.

The angry color left Rosemary's cheeks. In a normal voice, she said, "Yes, thank you, Daniel."

"My pleasure." He returned to his chair. Jo concentrated on picking up the last couple of fallen items. When she turned around, she saw he'd topped up her glass. She sipped it and felt her nerves steady.

Nan was busy looking through her notebook. "I knew it," she said triumphantly. "You're marrying my granddaughter."

Tension locked Jo's spine.

"I want to," said Dan. "She hasn't agreed yet."

"Making him wait, eh? I led your grandfather a merry dance, too." Rosemary's gaze fell on the clock. "Oh, my goodness, look at the time. He'll be home soon from the paper and I haven't started dinner." She bustled to her feet. "Jocelyn will look after you, Daniel, but no more picking my raspberries, you rascals. I want them for jam." Putting her empty champagne glass in her handbag she left the room.

In her wake there was complete silence. Even Vince had run out of croon. "So," Jo said, "still want to get hitched?"

DAN TOOK A MOMENT to collect himself. "I had no idea she'd gotten this bad."

"Nan was always very clear that she didn't want her deterioration broadcast." Jo put her glass on the mantel. "Only close friends know."

That stung. "I'm a close friend."

"You stopped being a confidante when you started trying to bulldoze me into marriage."

"Don't give me that," he said harshly. "This must have been going on for months."

Jo hesitated. "I figured you had enough on your plate this past year," she admitted.

No wonder she was looking so goddamn tired. Dan stood up and opened his arms. "Come here." When she shook her head, he added, "For ten minutes we'll revert to friends."

She looked as though she wanted nothing more than to lay her head on his shoulder, but Jo shook her head again. "Thanks, but I'll wait until normal service is resumed."

A thought occurred to him. "Is *this* why you won't marry me? You know I'll do anything for Nan."

"Stop," she said in exasperation. "I'm not marrying you because we don't love each other, remember?"

"Yeah, we do, and before you get hung up on the hearts and flowers and starry-eyed bullshit that burns out in a couple of months, answer me this. Has any romantic relationship come close to what we've got? Seriously, Jo, what other guy could understand you better than I do?"

"That used to be true," she said drily. "Before this week. Now I'm thinking we've mostly lived in different places for ten years, and you don't know me at all."

God, he loved a challenge. "Yeah? Take a seat, Ms. Swann, because this is your life."

"Go ahead," Jo sat down and crossed her legs. "Amaze me."

"I know at thirteen you loved New Kids on the Block and had a crush on Donnie Wahlberg. And now you've ditched him for his actor brother, Mark." As her lips curved he added, "And that the easiest way to defuse an argument is to make you smile."

She pursed her lips.

"I know that you thrive on opposition, believe politics should be clean, the world just and the environment protected."

"All public knowledge," she countered. "Especially Mark Wahlberg."

Dan leaned forward. "I know the *Chronicle* is your pride and joy but sometimes it feels like an albatross around your neck." She blinked. "I know you want kids because you grew up without siblings, and for some reason you're now pretending you don't." Jo shifted in her chair. "I know it's not commitment that scares you, but claustrophobia because I feel the same way. And that we're friends because we give each other room to breathe."

Her eyes widened and he felt equally surprised. Some of this was news to him, too. "I know," he said slowly, "you wonder if your relationships fail because you're too independent. But it's because you've been dating the wrong guys. The ones who act tough but whose masculinity is threatened by a woman who can take care of herself." They stared at each other. Dan tried to remember where he was going with this. That's right, talking her into marrying him.

"All that makes you a good friend," said Jo, "but there's no spark, Dan. I didn't feel anything when I kissed you in Auckland and neither did you. You were horrified."

"Because I was getting a hard-on with someone I'd only ever thought of as a friend," he said bluntly.

"You were as relieved as hell when I said it wasn't about you."

"I was shipping out the next night. I didn't have time to deal with it."

"Be honest, none of this would have come up again if you hadn't been through a tragedy."

He frowned. "Does it matter how we got

here? You say you didn't feel a spark when we kissed. Let's verify that."

She swallowed. "You mean kiss?"

He remembered that night in Auckland. Her breasts, the see-through top, remembered her bold tongue. "Unless you've got a better offer?"

She ignored that. "And if there's no spark on my side, you'll back off this wedding?"

"Yes." He hadn't participated in that kiss; this one he was definitely getting involved. And Dan knew how to please women.

"Fine." She stood up, gestured for him to do the same. Before he'd fully straightened, she'd pressed a quick kiss on his lips and stepped back. "Like I said, nothing."

"Nice try, Swannie."

She sighed. "You mean a kiss kiss?"

He knew not to smile. "I mean a kiss kiss."

"No groping...we're talking first base."

He ran teasing fingers over her forearm. "Just to be clear on the green zones. This okay?"

She frowned. "Quit making fun and let's get this over with."

His fingers continued stroking up the angora sleeve, over her shoulder and closed around the bare nape of her neck.

As he bent closer, Jo's eyes grew wary. Nervously, she closed them and braced herself. Dan kissed her, angling his mouth over hers with gentle pressure. Her lips tightened. Under his hand, her neck tensed. Dammit, he needed this to work. Cupping her face with his free hand, he coaxed her resistant lips apart with his tongue. She tasted good, smelled good...if only she'd relax into it. But Jo remained wooden in his arms.

Now he knew how she'd felt kissing him.

Frustrated, he broke contact. "This only counts if you kiss me back."

They tried again. Reluctantly her tongue touched his, withdrew, then came back, tentative and sweet. Vulnerable in a way he'd never associated with her. It caught him off guard. Made him feel—

Jo broke free. "Dan, I'm sorry." She wiped her mouth with the back of her hand. "But this is too weird."

Stunned, he removed his hand from the nape of her neck. "In that case," he rasped and she glanced up hopefully. Dan stopped. Her irises were like thin bands of predawn gray around a black horizon.

He stroked his thumb along that stubborn jawbone and Jo's pupils flared wider. "Nothing, huh?"

"Not a thing."

"Your pupils are dilated," he said.

"What?"

"It's an involuntary sexual response."

Her lashes fell and she moved away. "That's *one* reason pupils dilate. There must be others."

Dan followed her. "Well, yeah, you could be a drug addict or have accidentally ingested jet fuel or contracted rabies."

She turned on him. "Look, this is ridiculous, I don't fancy you. End of story. Now call off the bloody wedding."

Something didn't add up. "Why are you so resistant?"

"I had coffee with your mom today. She's worried about you."

Dan tried not to stiffen. "It's one of her hobbies."

"*I'm* worried about you. Pat said you're not sleeping, working too hard—"

"For the last time, I have *not* got post-trau-matic stress disorder."

"No, you haven't," she agreed.

He eyed his best friend warily. "But?"

"But you're still grieving and you've got it into your head that marrying me is the way through it."

"That's bullshit. I'm prioritizing what's im-portant to me and—"

"Hear me out. Please." Jo took his hands,

her expression serious. "You and I have been friends forever, it's natural we fall back on each other in hard times. Maybe make more of our friendship than we should. But your grief will pass, Dan, and so will these feelings for me. Then we'll be friends again." She smiled. "And you'll meet someone you really want to marry, have multiple children and I will dance at your wedding."

"To what?"

"Excuse me?"

"What song are you dancing to?" he inquired. "When you're imagining my wedding to someone else?"

Her smile faded. "Let's stick to the point."

"Humor me."

Jo's eyes narrowed. "The chicken dance."

He smiled. "I'll make sure it's on our playlist."

She dropped his hands. "Think about it, Dan. The other day you said you wanted to live big for Steve and Lee—shouldn't this be about us?"

"You're right." He managed to keep his tone even. "That's why I'll be seeing you in the morning."

Jo saw by his face that she'd struck a nerve so she didn't argue. Instead she closed the door quietly behind him and rested her forehead against it. With her whole heart she wanted to give Dan the comfort he needed, but that wasn't in either of their best interests right now.

Especially given her unexpected response to his kiss. It had taken everything she had not to kiss him back. God, no, she thought despairingly. Why did she have to want him now?

At the sound of approaching footsteps she straightened. When Polly entered the room, Jo was clearing the champagne flutes.

"Rosemary's settled in the conservatory with her jam-making recipes," said the nurse. "There's a shepherd's pie in the oven for dinner."

"Thanks, Pol, I don't know what I'd do without you."

"He asked me how I knew you."

Jo paused. "What did you say?"

"I made something up. Jo, why did you never tell him the truth?"

With a sigh, Jo gestured to a chair and Polly sat down. Pouring the nurse a glass of champagne, she picked up her own but didn't drink, absently watching the bubbles rise through the pale straw-colored liquid. "He'd take Nan on in a heartbeat, you know that? He didn't even flinch. But then Dan's always shouldered more than his fair share of responsibility. Walking his little sisters to school, minding them at home.

He was always the go-to guy for our friends. He said to me once, 'You're the only person I never worry about, do you know how restful that is?'"

"And if you told him that will change?"

She said slowly, "I think if I saw pity in his eyes I'd shoot him and then myself." Jo put down her glass. "I know it's not rational, but I've always needed him to see me as someone as strong as he is. It got me through a lot this year." She shrugged. "Something has to stay the same, you know?"

The other woman nodded, sympathy in her gaze and Jo looked away. "Anyway, this isn't about me. Dan lost two of his mates last year.... I think this is really about coming to terms with his mortality."

Polly winced.

"Exactly," said Jo and stood up. "So, shepherd's pie you say?"

CHAPTER SEVEN

DAN PUSHED HIS MEAL around the plate, too aggrieved to do more than pick at his mother's excellent roast beef. He'd only accepted Pat's dinner invitation because she'd started complaining that Herman was getting all their son's "quality time" and Dan didn't want her thinking he was taking sides. And how had she repaid his loyalty?

With a knife in the back. He stabbed a portion of beef. "Can you please quit telling people I've got post-traumatic stress disorder?" he said curtly. "I wasn't even on patrol for f...flock's sake."

"It wasn't people," his mother corrected. "It was your best friend."

"What were you two meeting for, anyway?"

Pat took her time finishing a mouthful of baby peas. "She's worried about you...and your strange behavior over this wedding. So are your father and I."

Herman raised his eyes from his roast

potatoes, met Dan's hard stare and dropped them again. "Let them sort it out," he advised his wife.

"You mean do nothing and hope the problem will go away," Pat returned. Silverware chinked against china as she put down her fork. "Danny, will you please tell your father you can manage August ewe vaccinations without his assistance? We'll miss the whole northern summer at this rate."

It was Dan's turn to receive a hard-eyed stare from Herman. How the hell did he end up monkey in the middle again? "I'm staying out of your private life, Mom," he reminded her, hacking through a dinner roll. "In fact, maybe you could take a lesson from that. And quit deflecting—I'm the injured party here."

He pointed his knife accusingly at her as he continued. "You don't want me to marry Jo so you engineered a get-together to sow more doubts in her mind. As if I don't have enough to deal with already, without you adding new ones."

Angry color flagged Pat's cheeks. She leaned forward, her pearls swinging dangerously over the gravy boat. "If you must know, Jo organized the meeting to tell me she isn't marrying you."

Dan's sense of ill use grew. "I'm guessing you two really bonded over that."

"I have to say I liked her more than I ever have." Pat sat back and picked up her cutlery. "She has no intention of taking advantage of your emotional fragility."

"My *what?*" Okay, now he was *really* pissed. "I've spent the past five days trying to get that woman to take advantage of me. Now you've taken me back to square one with this psycho-babble bullsh—"

"Son," Herman warned. Mouth trembling, Pat looked down at her plate.

"Mom, I'm sorry," he said curtly. "I know you believe that stuff." As an apology it sucked but right now it was the best he could manage.

"I only want you to be happy," she said in a small choked voice.

"I know you do, but—"

"And self-help books *can* be transformational." Dan hid his incredulity. "I gave Jo a wonderful book called *Contented Dementia* but she accidentally left it behind."

Accidentally, my ass. "What a shame."

"I'll get it and you can drop it off in the morning when you're trimming the hedge." As soon as she left the dining room, Dan and Herman exchanged a look.

"You two better not be rolling your eyes in

there," Pat called. Returning with the book, she laid it by Dan's plate. "It wouldn't do you any harm to read it, either."

How had they got off topic again? "Just promise you'll keep your opinions on my so-called emotional fragility to yourself in future," he said irritably. "And you're supposed to be on *my* side."

Pat snorted as she took her seat. "You can talk, Daniel Jansen. You said you'd stay a neutral party in my battle with your father over Italy and yet you're constantly enabling him."

"Enabling?" Dan looked to Herman for an explanation but his father's expression was vacant. *See no Pat, hear no Pat, speak no Pat.* Honestly, these two were as bad as each other.

"Letting him spend all his time at the farm," Pat explained. "How am I supposed to pry him out of the rut when you're making it comfortable?"

Dan pushed his plate aside. "Is this about ewe vaccination? Just because I'm not pinning Dad down to a handover date, Mom, doesn't mean I'm taking his side. We never talk about Italy." Again he glanced at his father, who kept stolidly eating.

"Exactly," Pat exclaimed. "You're *enabling* his avoidance. If you're not part of the solution,

Dan, you're part of the problem. At least I try to help you where I can."

"Oh, for God's sake." He'd had enough. "Dad, make Mom happy and set a departure date. And forget about the farm's calendar. I can always employ contractors if I need to."

"In case you haven't noticed," said Herman, "I seem incapable of making your mother happy."

Great, now he was in a snit.

"Incapable?" Pat sniffed. "Unwilling more like."

Herman threw down his napkin. "I had this town house built for you, didn't I? Wait a minute...wasn't *that* supposed to make you happy?"

Pat's eyes flashed. "Don't take that hard-done-by tone with me. You know it was only the first stage of our retirement plan. And what's the point of this place anyway, if you're hardly here?"

"Okay, you're talking now," Dan ventured cautiously. "Keeping the communication lines open...that's good isn't it, Mom?"

She ignored him in favor of glaring at his father. "Herman, if you don't set a retirement date right now—"

It was like watching two locomotives steaming toward a head-on a collision. "Venus and

Mars, Mom," he reminded her. "You know men don't respond well to ultimatums."

"Well, Herman?" Pat said in her dangerous voice.

Dan swung his attention to his father. "Dad, make a concession."

Instead Herman folded his arms and jutted out that stubborn Dutch chin. "Patricia, this isn't the way forward."

"As long as I'm moving, I don't care anymore," Pat cried. "I'm so sick of this standing still."

"C'mon, Dad, you can do it. Cut the hot wire." Defuse the *goddamn bomb*.

Instead his father broke the most basic rule of *Understanding Women 101*. He shrugged.

Dan dropped his head in his hands and waited for the detonation.

"I want a divorce," snarled his mother.

MUFFLED THUDS JARRED Jo awake. Still half-asleep, she crawled out of bed and opened her bedroom door. "Nan?" Light spilled into the hall from the spare room. Her grandmother was up again. As she staggered down the hall, there was another, louder thud. "Nan!" Jo surged into the room, blinking against the light.

Rosemary wrestled with the catch of a

large trunk, normally stored at the top of the wardrobe. "Help me open this."

Her adrenaline now ebbing, Jo stifled a yawn. "It's the middle of the night." And the third late night in a row.

"Nonsense," said Rosemary. "It's only just got dark."

Humoring her was the quickest way back to bed. Jo freed the catch on the trunk.

"Are you looking for more jumble?" For many years Rosemary had run the church's charity shop. As her memory faded, she'd begun filling plastic bags with her own clothes, then Jo's, getting snippy when her granddaughter returned everything to the wardrobe. Finally Jo had the bright idea of keeping old clothes in a heap on the spare bed.

"Jumble…no! I'll never give this away." Nudging Jo aside, Nan opened the lid, tossing out old linen and lace tablecloths until, with a cry of triumph, she uncovered a flat bundle swathed in silver tissue paper. Carefully she unwrapped a dress, holding it against herself as she turned to the old-fashioned swing mirror.

"Oh, Nan, it's beautiful." The ivory gown had a fitting crossover bust and cascading skirt— smooth satin overlaid with filmy chiffon—and the waist panel sparkled with beads.

"Swarovski crystal. I sewed on every one by hand. Someone's getting married… Is it me?"

With a sinking feeling, Jo recalled where she'd seen the dress before. Nan and Pops's grainy black-and-white wedding photos. "No one's getting married."

Her grandmother struggled with the bodice's zip. "I'd better try it on."

Jo gestured to the mirror so Nan could see the difference between her own mature figure and the narrow-waisted gown. "It won't fit anymore."

Rosemary looked between herself and Jo, then her face cleared. "That's right, I got it out for you."

Of all the things for her to remember. "I'm not marrying Dan."

Rosemary's brows rose in surprise. "You're marrying Daniel? Why didn't you tell me?"

"Because I'm not marrying him."

Her grandmother looked confused. "All right, dear, no need to snap."

"Sorry." Jo rubbed her gritty eyes. "Can we please go back to bed now?"

Nan stroked the silk fabric. "You know, I made this dress. Sewed every bead on by hand. Hours and hours it took. I'll never forget Graham's face when he saw me. We were a good team. He had the book sense and I had the common sense."

"What a lovely story," Jo said, though she'd heard it a thousand times. How Nan met Pops at a weekly dance where he'd been dragged by friends. How she'd fallen for the quiet intellectual struggling to set up the *Chronicle*. Pops wrote impassioned editorials and championed local causes; Nan found advertisers and made sure they paid on time.

"My goodness," she added, "it's two o'clock in the morning. Time to hit the sack."

Ignoring Jo's hint, Nan sat on the spare bed, absently picking up a straw hat that lay among the old clothes. "Do you know how I came to be in New Zealand?"

"You can tell me in the morning."

"My friend Mary had a brother here." Putting on the hat, Nan settled back against the headboard, placing the wedding dress across her knees like a blanket. "I met her when I was a land girl—farming in the Women's Land Army—during the war. You can't imagine—"

"Nan," Jo interrupted. "You don't want to crush that beautiful wedding dress. Shall I put it away?"

Rosemary looked at the gown in surprise. "Now, why did I get this out? Oh, yes, someone's getting married." She thrust it toward Jo. "Try it on."

"Only if we go straight to bed afterward."

"Whatever you want," Nan said reasonably.

Turning her back, Jo shrugged off her nightgown and pulled on the dress on over her underwear. Even swaying with fatigue, she handled the delicate fabric gently. Her grandmother swung into professional gear, coming over to smooth the short lace sleeves and straighten the folds across the bodice.

Rosemary struggled with the zip—they gave her trouble now—but Jo knew not to rush her and eventually the zipper slid up her back. As Nan's hands brushed along her bare skin, Jo shivered.

"Your hands are freezing." Picking up a blanket, she draped it around her grandmother's shoulders.

"Yes, yes, never mind that." Clutching the blanket, Nan stepped back for a better view. "I *knew* it would suit you," she said with satisfaction.

Jo turned to the mirror and felt her throat tighten. The slim-fitting dress folded beautifully over the bustline in a V that hinted at cleavage. Lacy sleeves added a touch of whimsy and the skirt flowed over her hips in a waterfall of satin and silk that contrasted with the nipped waistline and glittering crystals. Tears pricked her eyes.

Rosemary's face fell. "Is something wrong?"

"No, it's just so beautiful."

"I sewed on every bead by hand."

"Really? You are so clever." She hugged the old lady, dislodging her hat. Nan straightened it.

"Of course, Jo, we'll have to do something about your hair."

Over Nan's shoulder, Jo took another look in the mirror and laughed. Her curls corkscrewed in all directions, dark circles gave her a panda look and her pallor would have suited the bride of Frankenstein. "Maybe we should get some beauty sleep?"

"Good idea." Freeing herself from the hug, Rosemary left the bedroom with a little wave. "Sleep tight."

"Um, can you unzip me first?"

"Happy to help." Her grandmother re-entered the room and started fumbling with the zip. "It seems to be a little stuck." Jo was jerked backward.

"Be careful of the dress."

For a few more minutes Nan struggled. "I don't think…for heaven's sake…what's wrong with it?" Another jerk. She was getting upset.

"You know what?" Jo stepped away. "I might keep this on a bit longer."

"Yes, I think that's best," Rosemary said, relieved. "I don't want to tear it."

Jo tucked her grandmother's arm in hers. "Let's get you to bed."

"I am very tired," she confided.

"Well, you work so hard."

"I like to be busy. And tomorrow I'm making jam. The raspberries are in season." Jo made no comment. Outside the window, autumn rain lashed the pane.

In Nan's bedroom, Jo pulled back the blankets on the bed and her grandmother lay down with a sigh. Jo removed her shoes but Nan balked at the hat. "A lady likes to look her best."

"Very true." The silk of the wedding dress rustled as Jo bent to tuck her in and kiss her cheek.

Nan smiled. "Snug as a bug in a rug."

She'd said that every night through Jo's childhood. They held each other's gaze in a rare moment of communication, then Rosemary snuggled into the pillow.

"I love you, Nan," Jo whispered.

"Goodnight, Lizzie."

After a moment of shock, Jo went to her bedroom. Bending and twisting, she struggled to unzip the dress. It didn't budge. Looking over her shoulder in the mirror she saw that the chiffon overlay had snagged. This joke was getting funnier and funnier.

Resisting the urge to tear and rip she told her reflection not to panic. "Polly's pulling extra duty tomorrow. She'll get it off."

Jo lay down on her single bed, smoothing out the skirt before she pulled up the covers. Normally she slept curled on her right side. Fortunately, she was too damned miserable to quibble about things like comfort.

Her mother, Lizzie Swann, had been an only child, wild and impetuous. She'd run off with a married man when she was nineteen. Two years later she'd come home from Australia with a baby daughter.

Jo had no recollection of her mother, who'd died when she was two, but Nan and Pops's love had more than filled the gap. The Swarovski crystals pressed into her back and she turned on her side.

Goodnight, Lizzie.

It was the first time Nan had confused who she was.

The first time in her life she'd felt like an orphan.

CHAPTER EIGHT

AT FIVE-THIRTY IN THE MORNING WHILE Dan was sitting at the table scrutinizing farm records, Herman, dressed for farm work, walked into the kitchen and grunted hallo. Then his father opened the back door, hauled on work boots and disappeared into the dawn, whistling for the dogs.

"Great," Dan said to his ledger. "Just bloody great." Getting up, he closed the door. Blue crawled out from under the kitchen table, where he'd been warming Dan's feet, and looked up at him with plaintive eyes, ears cocked.

Dan sighed. "Et tu, Brute?"

Blue whined. "Fine." Dan opened the door. "As long as you can square it with your conscience." Without a backward glance, the old dog tore off after Herman's receding back. Dan cursed. He could just see how this was going to play out. A brooding Herman killing himself with young man's work while Mom sat by the phone in her town house waiting for a call his pig-headed father was too proud to make.

"Like hell." Dragging on his own work boots, Dan followed his father to the lit barn where he found him loading feed sacks on the back of the ATV. "Go see Mom and sort this out. You know she didn't mean it."

After her demand for a divorce last night, Pat had thrown them out. Herman headed for the whiskey bottle as soon as they'd returned to the farmhouse. His big mouth had caused enough trouble for one night, so Dan had made up the single mattress in the spare room for his father and slunk off to his new bed where he was so desperate for distraction from his compounding troubles that he'd read *Contented Dementia*… It was surprisingly good.

Herman threw some rope over the sacks to tie them in place. "Maybe I want her to mean it."

Dan stopped fondling Blue's ear. "What?"

"Maybe I'm tired of being the bad guy." Herman jerked the rope tight. "Tired of everything that's wrong with our marriage being my fault." Another loop, another jerk. "She says she needs to be needed…complains that I don't share my feelings." Herman tied a knot that only a knife would sever. "Would you show your underbelly to someone who holds you accountable for everything that goes wrong in her life?"

"But you love her, Dad." Mom might not see it but her son did.

"And what's it worth? *Niks.*" His father always defaulted to Dutch words when he was upset. "Everything we've built together over thirty-five years—a farm, a family—none of that means anything compared to the life Pat could have had if she hadn't married me. I've worked my fingers to the bone to give that woman every-thing she missed out on, and none of it matters. Whether we're in Tuscany or Timbuktu, I'm never going to be enough for her."

"Dad," Dan said softly.

"*Nee,* son." His father's voice was thick with pain and bitterness. "If your mother wants to lose the deadweight holding her back, let her, eh?"

He started up the ATV's engine, forestalling further argument, gestured the dogs on the back and sped off.

Dan packed up his pruning tools and chain-saw and drove to the Swann house. He'd make a start on the hedge with hand clippers until the household woke up because he sure as hell couldn't stay around here watching Herman suffer.

He hadn't expected anyone up at six, but he met Rosemary at the front gate, on the verge of going for a walk. "Daniel, what a nice surprise."

"We arranged it yesterday."

She looked at him blankly. Dan recalled the book he'd read last night and tried again. "I thought I'd trim the back hedge for you."

"Oh, good, it's been annoying me. Come in." Chatting about the garden, she led the way into the house.

Except for that initial forgetfulness, she seemed her old self today with none of the confusion that characterized her yesterday. And nothing about her appearance was out of the ordinary. She wore pants, a neat blouse and a fleecy gray cardigan.

Inside, she surprised him by patting his cheek. "You're a good boy, Daniel. I never worry about Jo when she's with you." Dan swallowed a sudden lump in his throat. He believed he was doing the right thing with this wedding but encouragement was in short supply. Yet this woman had always given it to him.

"Great handshake, Daniel," she'd approved when Jo first brought her five-year-old classmate home. "Firm. And you look me in the eye. Excellent. You can always tell the quality of a man by his handshake, his posture and his shoes."

Dan had squirmed in embarrassment as

Rosemary's gaze dropped to his bare feet. "Except in this hot weather," she'd added smoothly, then kicked off her elegant pumps and wandered around for the rest of his visit in stocking feet. He'd adored her ever since.

Entering the kitchen, he saw the counter was covered with glass jars of all shapes and sizes. Over the back of a dining chair was an apron he remembered fondly from his childhood—hand-painted with bunches of red cherries.

"You're making jam today?"

"Yes, raspberry." Rosemary fumbled to put her apron on. "Let's go and pick some right now."

Except it was late autumn, not summer. As he tied the apron strings for her, Dan thought carefully. "I saw a lot of mandarins on the tree out front. I'd hoped you were making marmalade."

"You always did love my marmalade, didn't you? Well, if the mandarins are ready." Handing him a bucket, she led the way outside again, across the damp grass.

"I was a land girl in the war," she said as they started picking. "My job was to grow crops to feed our boys." She looked at him through the mandarin tree, her blue-gray eyes bright as a bird's through the dark green.

Dan smiled at her. "Yes, I know."

"Tell me, Daniel, are you still intending to join the army?"

And because it was Nan who'd known him since he was five and she wouldn't remember this conversation he said, "I don't think I'd make a good soldier anymore."

"My younger brother Georgie wanted to be a soldier." The fruit landed in the bucket with a soft thud. "He spent most of the war fretting that he'd miss the fun. He enlisted on his eighteenth birthday…January 5, 1945."

"That's when you want to join a war," Dan commented, "close to winning it."

Rosemary chuckled. She was picking carelessly, tearing the fruit off stems and leaving behind tufts of exposed inner rind, torn fragments of veined white. "Georgie loathed fruit and vegetables," she said. "He'd only eat potato. When I was chipping away at the frozen earth to plant the bloody things in Somerset I'd tell myself he needed them in Normandy."

She cupped a mandarin in her hand, as though trying to warm herself with it. "At least it was summer when he died. The soil would have turned more easily when they buried him." Nan dropped the mandarin on the grass. "You have to keep planting," she said, her voice as rusty as an old wheelbarrow, "you have to bring life back from the earth."

He caught her hands. "I'd like to grow fruit trees," he said, "but I'm not sure which fruit makes the best jam. I could really do with some advice."

He could almost see her coming back, her face breaking into a smile of relief as she recognized him. "Well," she said happily, "you've come to the right person. You can make good jam out of any fruit if you know the secret."

"Secret?" Picking up the bucket, Dan led her back to the house. His heart ached for Georgie, for Steve and Lee, for all the men who died in foreign lands.

"Methylated spirit…" Her eyes sparkled. "You use it to test for pectin. Take one spoon of boiling juice from the pan, then add three spoonfuls of meths when it's cool. If a large clot forms, then your jam will set well." They entered the kitchen. "You can put the mandarins in the pantry."

He hadn't been in the pantry since he was a kid. Dan found himself looking on the second shelf for the biscuit tin, caught himself and smiled.

"Is that Polly you're talking to?" he heard Jo say. "Pol, don't laugh but I tried Nan's wedding dress on last night and wouldn't you know it, the zip got stuck."

Intrigued, Dan walked out of the pantry. His

bride stood with her back to him, getting a glass of water, her short curls a riotous tumble and wearing a beautiful, if crumpled, gown.

"Isn't this bad luck before the wedding?"

Jo gasped and spun around. "You're early."

"You know what they say about the early bird." His appreciative gaze traveled down the dress and up again to Jo's blushing face. "Wow."

"Don't read anything into this," she warned.

"Actions speak louder than words." He remembered this feeling—optimism.

"Nan asked me to try it on and—"

"I did no such thing, young lady." Tutting, Rosemary started smoothing out the wrinkles. "Good heavens, it looks like you slept in it."

Jo's blush deepened. "And then I couldn't get it off."

Dan smiled. "I'll help you take it off."

She frowned at him as Rosemary tugged at the zip. "What on earth have you done here?" she scolded. "The chiffon's caught."

Or maybe he'd leave it on, slide his hands down the silky fabric covering her delightful butt, then lift that pretty skirt.... "Would you like me to try?" Dan suggested meekly.

"No!"

"Good idea." Rosemary propelled her reluctant granddaughter closer.

Jo turned her back on him. "I mean it," she muttered. "This has absolutely no connection with us." The blush even tinted her neck. He wanted to bite it.

"Uh-huh."

The dress smelled of lavender, the silk felt blood-warm. The back cut away to a modest V but he still had to fight the impulse to lean forward and lick the smooth skin it exposed. Dan took his time freeing her. This was the longest he'd been this close to her since his return and he made the most of it. Jo squirmed under his caressing fingers.

"Don't fidget," said Rosemary, hovering anxiously. "You'll tear it."

"Listen to your grandmother," said Dan, enjoying himself immensely. Rosemary nodded her approval.

"You know, I sewed every bead on by hand. Hours and hours it took. I'll never forget Graham's face when he saw me." In Nan's face, Dan caught a glimpse of the young bride she'd once been. Jo nodded but tensed. How many times, he wondered, had she heard this story? He lifted his hands to her shoulders in silent support, all teasing gone.

Rosemary was still talking. "His family never thought I was good enough but we were a great team. You two make a great team, too. I've always thought so."

Jo moved away from his hold. "Nan, we're not getting married."

"And when she's with you, Daniel, I never worry. Now…what was I…?" Her voice trailed off; her attention turned inward. Her hands fluttered around her apron as though searching for a hold; she looked down at the cherries printed on it and her face cleared.

"I'm making jam today."

"The mandarins for the marmalade are in the pantry," he reminded her.

"Excellent." Rosemary bustled into the larder. Dan returned to untangling Jo's zip.

"She was up in the night and wouldn't settle until I tried it on," said his bride defensively. "I haven't changed my mind about marrying you."

"You know what I think?"

"I know I'm not going to like it."

He freed the last of the delicate fabric and pulled the zipper down slowly. "Your subconscious is on my side." He brushed his lips along the bumps in her spine.

Jo jumped and tried to tug away. "No, it's not."

Holding the opened zip, Dan smiled at the

goose bumps his kiss had raised. "And so is your body." She bowed her head. "Jo?"

Rosemary staggered out of the pantry with the bucket of citrus. Releasing the dress, Dan went to help. "Daniel, how nice of you to visit," she exclaimed. "You knew I was making your favorite marmalade, didn't you?"

"I could never sneak anything past you, could I?" Taking the bucket, Dan turned back to Jo.

She was gone.

JO STOOD AT HER BEDROOM window, watching Dan wield a chainsaw, slicing through the tangled hedge like it was a pat of soft butter. Why couldn't he simply accept her refusal? Why did he have to persist with this ridiculous wedding deadline? She didn't want to humiliate him.

When she'd finally fallen asleep she'd dreamed of him standing in the church, waiting for her, his expression drawn and anxious. The congregation's whispers becoming titters, then laughs until everyone howled. She'd woken up crying.

In a stupid wedding dress.

With a sigh, Jo returned it to storage, repacking it in tissue and laying the stalks of dried lavender through the folds to protect it. It was a battle of nerves and she had to win for the sake of a friendship neither of them could afford to lose.

She glanced out the window again, this time at her grandmother, sitting in an armchair in the glass conservatory adjoining the kitchen where she was "supervising the work." Rosemary had dozed off—God knows how with that racket—but she was sleeping so little at night now. Picking up a blanket, Jo went downstairs and laid it gently over her knees. Nan didn't stir. In repose she looked like she always had.

Polly poked her head in and Jo raised a finger to her lips. Closing the door gently behind her, Jo returned to the kitchen.

"Tea?" suggested Polly.

"Coffee please." Jo yawned. Lately she existed on the stuff.

While Polly set up the coffeemaker, Jo eyed the bucket of mandarins, then with a shrug found a couple of bowls and started slicing them.

The chainsaw stopped. Glancing through the kitchen window, she saw Dan taking an armful of clippings to the compost heap behind the shed. He'd taken off his jacket and his damp navy T-shirt clung to the muscles of his back. She remembered the touch of his lips on her neck and shivered.

"How long are you going to keep doing this

to yourself?" Polly found clean cups in the dish-washer. The smell of fragrant coffee mingled pleasantly with sharp-sweet citrus.

"He'll give up eventually."

"I'm not talking about Dan," said Polly, "I'm talking about Rosemary. How many nights this week has she been up?"

Jo scraped a sliced mandarin into a bowl, then reached for another. "I'm coping."

"Are you?" Polly picked up her hand holding the knife. She was trembling with exhaustion. "How many, Jo?"

She pulled her hand free. "A few," she admitted and concentrated on slicing.

Polly folded her arms, her expression set to charge nurse. "We talked about this."

"Let's see how next week goes." Her slices were getting thicker and thicker. "It could be a passing phase."

"You made a commitment," Polly said quietly.

The mandarin fell open; Jo gouged out the pips. "Look, I haven't got the energy to discuss this now." *No, don't reinforce Polly's argument.* "I mean, I'm too busy with the *Chronicle*." She and Kev were spending hours analyzing Comm-Link's annual reports and cross-checking profit forecasts with actual performance. Trying to work out whether CommLink was bluffing by a process of deduction. Because thanks to Dan, Kev no longer trusted Jo's instincts. She'd begun to question them herself.

"You promised me," repeated Polly. "And more importantly, you promised Rosemary."

Something inside Jo snapped. She threw down the knife. "If you haven't got the guts to see this through, Pol, then quit! I can do this alone."

"Ha," the nurse retorted. "You're so damn tired you're delusional!"

"Oh, God, I'm sorry." Jo gripped the table edge. "You know I don't mean it. You're the best thing that happened to both of us."

"Then listen to my advice. You *can't* continue like—"

"What's going on?" Dan said casually. Neither of them had heard the back door open. Arranging himself next to Jo, he glanced from one woman to the other. "I could hear you arguing from the garden."

Jo sent Polly a warning look. "We're discussing the best way to make marmalade."

The older woman shook her head. "I'm sorry, Jo, but I need reinforcements." She faced Dan. "When Rosemary was first diagnosed she chose a residential facility and had herself put on a waiting list for a place there when she needed full-time care."

"Polly, stop there." Jo tried to sound calm and authoritative but her heart hammered against her ribs.

"When the time came, Jo increased my hours instead," said the nurse. "I only found out when Pinehill phoned last month to see how things were progressing. Apparently Rosemary even made Jo promise to respect her wishes in front of the director."

Jo went to the sink and rinsed her juice-covered hands. "She's not a burden," she said to no one in particular.

"When I challenged her, Jo talked me into another deadline." Polly continued to look at Dan. "Once Rosemary was getting up through the night more than once a week, then Jo would accept the need for residential care. I suspect that's been happening for some time."

"She raised me. I'm not turning my back on her now."

"Someone needs to talk some sense into you before *your* health suffers," Polly said to her.

Jo concentrated on drying her hands but said fiercely, "I'm coping."

Polly picked up her bag. "We need more sugar from the store if we're making this marmalade. Anything else you want me to pick up?"

Yeah, a new caregiver. Jo bit her tongue against the sarcastic retort and shook her head.

This betrayal was exactly why she kept her own counsel. She waited until Polly was out of ear-shot and snarled at Dan instead. "This is none of your business."

"You're right," he agreed. "Any chance of breakfast? I'm starving."

Surprised, Jo blinked at him. "There's eggs… a loaf in the breadbox."

He opened the fridge, taking out the eggs, butter. "You eaten yet?"

"Uh, no, not yet." *Has Nan?* "I'll be back in a minute." Rosemary was still sound asleep, her mouth slightly open like a child's. Jo stood for a moment composing herself. After a few deep breaths the sick feeling in the pit of her stomach receded. She returned to the kitchen. Dan had already greased the skillet with butter and was mixing eggs in a bowl with a little milk.

"There's some cheese and tomatoes," she said, "if you prefer an omelet."

"Scrambled's fine. Got any parsley?"

"Tons." Jo went out to the overgrown garden. The parsley patch had rioted through summer; now in autumn it had gone to seed. She was mixing her seasons up as badly as Nan. But she found some spring onions that hadn't been har-vested and took them inside. Soon the pungent green onion mingled with the scent of buttery eggs. Jo realized she was hungry.

"I'll make toast," she suggested.

"Good idea."

She sent him a sidelong glance as she dropped two slices of wholemeal bread into the toaster. Maybe he was biding his time, lulling her into a false sense of security.

"Relax." His back to her, Dan stirred the eggs. "I'm not going to hassle you about Nan." He turned off the element; found plates and cutlery. "Polly doesn't know you like I do. Of course you know how to juggle multiple obligations, not to mention keeping yourself healthy." Jo concentrated on the toast. "You still jogging?"

"When I can fit it in." *Which is never.* She resisted the urge to check her reflection in the toaster.

"And Rosemary seemed fine when she let me in this morning. She was off for a walk but postponed it."

Jo's head shot up. She must have forgotten to dead-bolt the front door. The last time Nan had wandered they hadn't found her for three hours.

Dan glanced over. "Bread."

A wisp of smoke rose from the toaster. Jo rescued the toast and joined him at the table.

Her stomach had started churning again.

Dan picked up his knife and fork. "Mom asked Dad for a divorce last night."

"What!"

"I guess my appetite should be affected but frankly after missing dinner, I'm starving." He handed Jo her cutlery. "I told them I was sick and tired of acting as an intermediary and to sort out their own mess… That worked really well."

"Oh, Dan, I'm sorry." Stunned, Jo started to eat. "I'm sure Pat regrets what she said this morning."

"Dad doesn't." Between mouthfuls, he related his conversation with his father.

"Poor Herman. Yet I kind of understand where your mom's coming from. Your dad started this by reneging on a promise…and don't even try to bring this back to the promise I made to marry you. I was drunk."

Across the table, his eyes were very blue. "So both parties have to be sober for a promise to be binding?"

"Yes."

"Any other provisos?"

Jo covered her bases. "And both have to be serious when they make it. It should be witnessed. And preferably on paper…a legal document." That left out the beer mat.

Dan looked thoughtful. "Dad never signed anything promising Mom he'd travel. Theirs was only a verbal agreement."

She frowned. "Is that how he's trying to weasel out of it? No wonder Pat's had enough."

He sat back in his chair. "You really think he's bound by this, don't you?"

"Yes, I do," she said hotly. "Your mom trusted him and he's betraying that—"

Jo stopped, suddenly seeing the trap he'd laid for her. She put down her fork. "This isn't about your parents…or us, is it?"

Dan shook his head.

Jo pushed to her feet. The chair toppled to the floor. Throat tight, she flung open the back door. "Out…get out. If you really knew me you'd understand how I feel about Nan."

He stood. "I do understand. You want to fix this and it's driving you crazy that you can't. Which leaves you torn between respecting her wishes and hanging on to her for all you're worth."

She couldn't speak or she'd burst into tears. Holding the door open she blinked hard at the old-fashioned clock hanging on the opposite wall.

"Jo, you don't have to do this alone."

The second hand jerked around the clock face. "If you really want to help then cancel the wedding."

"I…can't. If I start letting you use delaying tactics we'll be eighty before we sort this out."

Still she wouldn't look at him. "Don't lecture *me* on accepting reality until you can."

He stopped in front of her, narrowing her view down to one muscular shoulder and a cord of bicep under the sleeve of his T-shirt.

"Sooner or later you're going to have to deal with the fact I'm serious about getting married. It would be nice if that happened before the wedding."

CHAPTER NINE

DAN QUASHED A FEELING of futility as he waited in the coffee shop for Delwyn later that day. He should have kept his mouth shut this morning instead of wading in on Rosemary's side but he couldn't stand by when he could plainly see that the status quo wasn't working. So he'd given his opinion and alienated the woman he wanted to marry in two and a half weeks.

He glanced at his watch. Five-thirty. Now even his wedding planner was standing him up. Lesser—or more intelligent—men would have taken that as a sign.

He'd give Delwyn five more minutes. An incurable romantic, she'd reassured him that she wasn't going to let Jo's threat of reprisal prevent her from furthering the cause of true love. And she was a mine of useful information. Thanks to Delwyn, Dan knew what needed to be organized, when, and with whom.

His cell beeped. To his relief it was a text from Jo. U were right. Book on dementia *was* good. Before he'd left, he'd told her she needed to read it. Nice to know she still gave him the benefit of the doubt in some areas. She'd got to it quickly, which only showed how desperate she was.

He texted back. I'll always be your friend, Jo.

It took a few minutes to get a reply. Ditto.

Dan couldn't help pushing his luck. Picking wedding rings tomorrow. Want to come?

Her reply was instantaneous. &*%#@

Smiling, he snapped the cell shut. Jo wanted a family. And she was a pragmatist, she had to see the advantage of what he was proposing, particularly since he'd proved they had a sexual attraction. He could help her care for Rosemary.

He pocketed his phone with the nagging feeling that he'd missed something in this puzzle. And time was running out.

Across the street, Delwyn hurried out of Tim's Auto Mechanics, her head down. Her fiancé worked there...what was his name? Skinny guy, hairy knuckles and a genius with diesel engines. Wayne.

"About time," Dan muttered, but instead of crossing the road, the plump sales rep turned left. She must have forgotten their meeting. As Dan went to the door to hail her, Wayne appeared at the garage doors in grease-stained overalls. Catching sight of Dan, he scowled and retreated into the gloom. What the hell was that about?

"Delwyn!" She spun around and Dan saw her puffy eyes, her red-tipped nose and quivering, blubbering mouth.

Uh-oh.

Delwyn crossed the road, her face crumbling, and he experienced a manly impulse to run. Ten yards away, she started to sob. Dan folded his arms. "What's wrong?"

"Wayne j-j-jilted meeee!"

It was a good ten minutes before Delwyn pulled herself together and by then everyone in the coffee shop was glaring at Dan as though he were an ax murderer. Ignoring them, he poured her a glass of water and slid it across the table.

"Okay, what happened?"

Elbows planted in a growing mound of crumpled tissues, Delwyn took a noisy gulp of water and wiped her eyes. "Last night I told Wayne I'd organized a makeover magic package." When he looked blank she waved an impatient hand. "That's a manicure, pedicure, waxing and bronzing treatment."

"Maybe he's worried about escalating costs... your coach and horses weren't cheap." Dan repeated his diplomatic reason for turning her down when she'd suggested they negotiate a two-for-one deal.

"Yeah, but I got a discount on the turtle-doves," she argued. "And anyway, you can't cut corners on your appearance on your wedding day." Delwyn sniffed. "The photos will be forever."

"I'm sure Wayne considers you beautiful as you are."

"It's not for me, it's for him!"

"You want to wax and manicure *Wayne?*"

"Don't sound so judgmental. It's only to get the grease out from under his fingernails, tidy his eyebrows and defuzz his back." She reached for another tissue and blew her nose. "It's not like I'm suggesting a Brazilian for heaven's sake… Well, okay, I did suggest it, but *Bridal* magazine said they're getting popular with guys. Of course they don't do it the same for men as for women. It's more like putting shapes in the hair." Delwyn's mouth drooped. "And a heart would have been nice."

Dan shook his head to dislodge the mental pictures. "C'mon, the guy's got a point."

"He didn't have to be so mean about it." she glowered. "Wayne said I'm a bridezilla who cares more about the wedding than about him. And that I'm no longer the carefree girl he fell in love with. But I am, Dan, I am!" She kicked the back of the booth.

"Okay," he said carefully. If he kept his mouth shut this time he wouldn't get into trouble.

Tears welled in her red eyes. "And Wayne said since he's not good enough as he is, I should find someone who m-matches my perfect day."

The poor bastard. Dan forgot his resolution. "Look, you can fix this. Go over and apologize for trying to change him."

Her mouth fell open. "Excuse me, *I'm* the victim here." Angrily, she wiped away her tears. "*I'm* the one who's spent the past six months weighing everything I eat. And all for a guy so selfish that he won't even try and improve. You know what? I'm *glad* I'm not marrying him." Her lower lip quivered. "But my wedding, Dan," she bawled, "my beautiful wedding."

Disgusted, he handed over another paper napkin and thanked God he wasn't marrying for love.

"I CAN'T BELIEVE Dan was so insensitive," Delwyn complained over the phone. "He ended up taking Wayne's side, can you believe it? You'll be pleased to know I'm not helping him marry you anymore."

You were still helping him? "I'm glad to hear it," Jo said mildly. By the light of the full moon, she was clearing the weeds around the gone-to-seed parsley. "Anyway, I'm sure you two will work something out."

Once the parsley was weed-free, she moved on to the mint. It was nice to be outside for a change, to feel the chill on her bare legs under her dressing gown, to smell the wet grass and admire the stars.

Nan had settled early tonight.

Aided by techniques suggested in *Contented Dementia,* it had taken Jo only thirty minutes to put her grandmother to bed, instead of the usual hour. She could see herself managing again.

"No," said Delwyn, "Wayne doesn't deserve me. You and I will be spinsters together." Jo heard a gulp.

She made a mental note to call in to the garage on her way to work and talk to Wayne.

Someone somewhere had a fire burning, she could smell it faintly on the breeze. Winter was coming with its late dawns and early dusks, with cold feet and a slap-you-awake chill when you stepped outside the house. Jo shivered. *I'm alive, alert, awake,* she reminded herself silently. And stopped before *enthusiastic.* Sighed. "Go to bed, Delwyn," she said. "Things won't seem so bad in the morning." *One day at a time, don't look too far ahead and you'll be okay.* They exchanged good-nights, Jo took in the stars one last time and turned back to the house. For a few seconds her brain couldn't process what she was seeing.

Through the downstairs window flames illuminated one corner of the dark kitchen. She started to run.

Inside, light flickered on the hall walls and smoke hung in the kitchen doorway like a gauze curtain. "Nan!" Bursting through it, Jo took in the room in one frantic glance.

The frying pan blazed with burning oil. Flames licked up the tiles behind the stove and around the edges of the range-hood. Three feet away from the fire, Rosemary was a wraith-like figure in her nightgown, poised to throw a jug of water.

"No!" Diving forward, Jo tackled her grandmother's legs. The plastic jug flew into the air, splattering water as they both fell heavily to the floor. A few drops hit the fire and it roared and shot higher.

Scrambling to her feet, Jo half dragged, half carried her grandmother into the hall. "You're hurting me," Rosemary whimpered.

"I'm sorry," Jo gasped, but didn't loosen her grip until she'd hauled the old woman to safety.

Propping Nan against the banisters, she wrenched open the fuse box and cut the power then raced back into the kitchen, raising her hand against the blast of heat. Jerking the fire extinguisher away from the wall she thrust it at the blaze and pulled the nozzle.

Nothing.

Jo shook the canister, then frantically pulled again. "Do something, do something!" Still nothing. On a sob she remembered the pin, fumbled to remove it and tried again. A shot of foam hit the fry pan. Smoke billowed.

Coughing and shaking, Jo swept the nozzle left to right, keeping it low. The fire died, but she kept spraying until nothing came out, then flung the canister away. Her legs gave way.

On hands and knees she crawled back to her grandmother. Rosemary lay curled on her side, cradling her left arm. "It's an air raid…get me into the shelter."

Jo smoothed her grandmother's tangled hair. "It's over," she rasped. "The all-clear's sounded. You're safe."

"My arm hurts."

"I'll get h-h-help." Teeth chattering—from the shock, she imagined—Jo went outside, found her cell where she'd dropped it and rang the emergency line as she raced inside. "I n-n-need…an ambulance."

As she gave the operator the address she pulled coats out of the closet and covered Nan, then sat beside her and stroked her frail back while her grandmother moaned and cried.

"It's okay, I'm here. Everything's going to be fine." Repeating the words over and over in a smoke-dry rasp until her voice cracked and faded.

Out of the dark, came a thin accusatory voice. "You broke my arm."

JO LET HIM HOLD HER; that's how devastated she was.

Dan kept his embrace gentle though he wanted to crush her into his very bones with the enormity of his relief.

Her head on his shoulder, they sat on the hospital sofa waiting while the doctors x-rayed and set Rosemary's arm, which Jo had broken during the tackle that saved the old lady's life. Oil and water didn't mix but Nan had forgotten that. Thank God Jo hadn't or they'd both be in the burns unit right now—or worse. His hold tightened.

Dan had coaxed Jo into showering and changing into the clothes he'd picked up at her request. His gut swooped remembering the kitchen—the charred wall behind the stove, the floor swimming in foam and black ash.

He'd opened all the windows before he left. Despite the shampoo, her damp hair still reeked of smoke. Dan resisted the urge to bury his face in it only by leaning his head against the wall so hard he could feel a bruise forming.

Jo stood up. Hands jammed in the pockets of her jacket, she walked up to the glass partition separating the small waiting room from the bustle of reception and scanned the corridor in both directions. "What's taking so long?" Her face was pale, the circles under her eyes smudged bruises.

"They want to do a good job."

"Yes, of course." She sat down again, taking the chair opposite. Withdrawing from comfort she felt she didn't deserve.

She had no reason to blame herself but she did. For relaxing her guard after settling Rosemary for the night. For being outside when her grandmother got up. For forgetting to turn off the master switch on the stove. "I'm being punished for not keeping my promise to Nan," she'd said when she phoned for his help.

She hadn't raised the subject since and neither had Dan. He understood Jo couldn't talk about this right now if she was going to hold herself together. Understood that was why she'd called him and not Polly.

"Are you staying overnight with her?" He kept his tone matter-of-fact.

She nodded. "And then at Pinehill until she

settles in." Jo dropped her gaze. "She can't go home with the house the way it is."

"Stay at the farm."

"No. You and Polly were right. It's time, Dan. I was selfish—I put my feelings before her personal safety.... Please don't disagree. It's true."

She wasn't going to listen, so he went and sat beside her, not touching her, just being there. After a few minutes, she lifted her head and forced a smile. "So, what's the latest on your folks?"

"Herman's still at the farmhouse." Casually he took her hand and warmed it between his. "Mom's saying she should have asked for a divorce years ago."

She entwined their fingers. "Do you think they're better off apart?"

"If they are, then I'm in trouble. Herman and I work fine together on a temporary basis but I'd run the place differently...no question." Hearing footsteps hurrying down the corridor, he paused. Jo's grip tightened. An orderly walked by without glancing in. "There is one good thing come out of their separation," Dan continued. "Dad's so grumpy that the dogs are finally changing loyalties."

Jo managed a weak chuckle and he felt like he'd won something.

"Jo?" Doc Stone entered the room and she shot to her feet. "All fine," he reassured her. "A simple closed fracture, it should heal without any trouble."

"Can I see her now?"

"Yes, of course, follow me."

Jo turned back to Dan. "You don't have to stay."

He hated to be shut out again. "Is there anything else I can do?"

Her gaze pinned his. "Only one."

Dan looked away. "Give Nan my love."

Without another word Jo followed the doctor. Dan loosened the fists in his pocket and headed out to the brightly lit parking lot.

She was angry and he didn't blame her. He should back off the wedding while she dealt with Rosemary. But he broke into a cold sweat even considering it. He felt like a marathon runner five miles out from the finish line. Putting one foot in front of the other. What happened at the tape, Dan had no idea.

Wearily he unlocked the ute and climbed into the cab. Jo might see any concession as a lack of resolve on his part. He couldn't risk that.

She'd called him tonight because no one in this world understood her better than he did.

When it mattered, they were always there for each other.

Hopefully she'd remember that on the day.

CHAPTER TEN

THREE DAYS LATER, from her position behind a beech tree, Jo listened to Nan conversing with Mrs. Smith. The two old women sat on a bench in front of the goldfish pond in Pinehill's half-acre garden. "You know the secret to setting jam?" said Nan. "Methylated spirits."

"I like a tipple myself," said Mrs. Smith. "Scotch and ginger ale...about five."

"Five? No, five pounds of sugar is too much... unless you're making double quantities."

The two lapsed into a companionable silence. It was a sunny day, warm enough to sit outside in this sheltered spot.

Jo became aware of bark scratching her cheek and jerked upright before she fell asleep. For seventy-two hours she or Polly had shadowed Nan through her transition to Pinehill, stepping in to troubleshoot when necessary.

"Do you think two hippos could share?" Mrs. Smith, who had big plans for turning Pinehill into a zoo, gestured to the goldfish pond. "I know it's only big enough for one but two would be company for each other."

"Yes, why not?" said Nan, plainly humoring her. "As long as they don't damage the trees."

Mrs. Smith opened the pictorial natural history book in her lap. "How do you feel about meercats?"

"I love cats. They stop rats nesting in the compost bin." Nan leaned forward and picked up her handbag, slinging it over the green fiberglass cast on her forearm. "Well, it's been lovely visiting but I must be getting home."

Jo trailed her grandmother into the L-shaped redbrick building, nodding to the supervising nurses' aid.

She hadn't approved when her grandmother chose Pinehill. As an outsider it had struck her as untidy and disorganized. Now Jo knew better. Cushions were strewn higgledy-piggledy because Mrs. Moreland, who'd been a window dresser, constantly rearranged them. And magazines lay open on every chair because Mr. Fairley, who'd been a newsagent, preferred them that way. Pinehill's philosophy was simple and effective. Every resident was treated as a trusted advisor on "how things should run around here."

Seeing how well Nan had settled in only deepened Jo's guilt.

Nan paused in front of the reception desk

where several nurses were in the middle of a shift handover. "You have too many flowers in your garden. You can't eat flowers."

One of them, Fiona, came out from behind the counter. "Perhaps you could give us some tips on starting a vegetable garden?"

Some of the hostility went out of Rosemary's tone. "Well, you need potatoes…but they can't be grown beside tomatoes…" She lost her train of thought. "Well," she said after a pause, "I must be getting home."

"What I'd really love to grow," commented Fiona, "is bananas."

Nan turned back. "Bananas are my favorite fruit. They weren't available through the war. Only apples and pears."

A bell rang from the dining room. Fiona looked at her watch. "It's twelve o'clock. How nice that you're here for lunch."

"Am I?" Rosemary looked uncertain.

"Yes, because I particularly need your advice. I'm having such trouble getting my jam to set." Fiona held out her arm.

Nan took it. "You know what my secret ingredient is?" she confided as they strolled toward the dining room. "Methylated spirit."

"We'll see you after breakfast tomorrow, then," called the charge nurse after Jo, who had begun to leave. It was time for her to drop back to daily visits, scheduled around Nan's most unsettled period.

"If she gets distressed…"

"We'll phone you, I promise. And you can ring us anytime, day or night."

"Thanks." Jo collected her overnight bag and walked outside. She felt like a mother leaving her child on the first day of school. Dan pushed himself off the verandah post.

"I told Polly I'd pick you up."

She should have been annoyed by his high-handedness in changing her arrangements, instead Jo felt pathetically grateful. Polly would have expected a postmortem. "Nan settled in really well," she said, smiling. "I don't know why I was so worried."

"That's great." Dan took her bag. "Since your kitchen's full of workmen, how about we get lunch before I drop you home?"

In the intensity of the past three days, she'd accepted his offer to organize repairs. At least workmen meant she wouldn't be going home to an empty house.

Jo hesitated.

"I'm not going to bring up the wedding," he said quietly.

"I wasn't worried about that," she lied. "And I'm fine about Nan now, honestly. Lunch would be great."

She'd eat, catch a nap and then go into the *Chronicle*. Bring herself up to speed for work tomorrow. With Nan getting settled at Pinehill, she could concentrate on CommLink again. Maybe it was being in an environment full of lateral thinkers but Jo now knew exactly how to find out whether Chris was bluffing. As she'd told Kev, it was simply a matter of looking at the problem from another angle.

Jo glanced at Dan. After CommLink she'd knock this crazy wedding scheme on the head once and for all.

"Shaker's okay?"

"Perfect. I'm in the mood for steak." Something not on the menu at Pinehill, which took into account its residents' increased difficulty with chewing and swallowing.

I hope someone's keeping an eye on Nan when she's eating.

"So," she said brightly. "What's been happening in the outside world?"

Dan shot her a sidelong glance then launched into a discourse on the latest skirmish between Labor and National over education policy. Slowly, Jo's anxiety dropped to a manageable level.

Over the entrée their debate about global warming grew heated; over dessert she wagered forty bucks on the All Blacks winning the Rugby World Cup and called Dan a traitor for favoring Australia's Wallabies.

He seemed tired, too, she noticed. Since he'd kissed her, she'd been scared to really look at him. Scared of seeing him differently. "How are Ross and Nate doing since Afghanistan?" she said over coffee. "We haven't had much opportunity to talk about them."

"Ross is driving himself too hard in rehab... but that's par for the course. Nate's resettled in the States. He's finding it hard to cope."

"I'm sure you all are."

"There's no comparison," he said curtly. "Ross and Nate were there—I wasn't."

She said slowly. "Do you think you could have changed the outcome? More likely you'd have been killed, too."

"Probably." He gestured for the waitress. "Listen, I should get back to the farm...Herman's in Auckland for a few days. And you need sleep."

"You're right," she admitted. "Even a double espresso isn't keeping me awake." She knew when she was being stonewalled. Would they ever get their easy friendship back? God, she hoped so.

Tradesmen's vans blocked her driveway. When Jo opened the passenger door, she was assaulted by a cacophony of buzz saws, hammering and an FM station blasting classic rock. "So much for a quiet nap."

"Why don't you come back to the farm? Herman's staying in Auckland for a stock auction and I'll be planting saplings along the creek. You'll have the place to yourself."

"I have to do this sooner or later," she said.

"You'll be better equipped after a couple hours of sleep."

That was true. "Okay," she said. "I'll check in with these guys, then follow in my car." No harm in having an escape vehicle.

The house smelled very faintly of smoke beneath the fresh paint and plaster. Inside the kitchen, plasterers were finishing the ceiling and walls around where the stove used to be. The tiles had been scoured clean, as had the rest of the kitchen. The singed countertops either side of the oven space had already been removed and the framing laid for the replacement counters.

"I can't believe the progress," she told the builder.

"Dan and Kev organized a working bee before we got here to clean the place up," he said. "Half of Beacon Bay showed up. The *Chronicle*'s helped a lot of community groups through the years."

She didn't know what to say. "It's all right,

love," the builder said gruffly. "You go on now, get some rest."

Jo didn't need telling twice. At the farmhouse she found a note taped to the front door. "Make yourself at home. Bed's made. Back around five."

Three hours. She'd make sure she was gone by then. Still, Jo hesitated before turning the handle. Bypassing his bedroom door she walked down the passage to the spare room. Clothes lay folded neatly on the bed and a bookmarked Tom Clancy novel lay on the floor beside it. Herman's space. Reluctantly Jo returned to Dan's bedroom.

She always teased him about his soldier's neatness but there was a heap of discarded clothes on the bedside table. Jo suspected they'd recently been on the floor because she found a sweater puddled behind the door when she closed it.

"Too busy planning this damn wedding," she muttered. Picking up the sweater, she hung it in the wardrobe.

He'd remade the bed with clean sheets; the old ones overflowed a laundry basket. The top corner of the duvet was turned back. His thoughtfulness brought dangerous emotions too close to the surface. Kicking off her trainers, Jo pulled off her sweater and, in her jeans and

T-shirt, crawled into the crisp sheets. The new mattress was just right.

Beneath the smell of laundry soap and fabric softener she caught the faintest hint of Dan's aftershave in the pillow. Jo closed her gritty eyes and slept.

SHE WOKE IN THE DARK, disoriented. Then, remembering where she was, she rolled over to look at the clock glowing on the bedside table—1:00 a.m.

Stunned, Jo fell back on the pillows. Dan must be in Herman's bed. She listened hard but heard nothing but the deep quiet of a country night. Pointless going home now; she might as well go back to sleep.

She clasped her hands behind her head and stared out the curtainless window. Nan was usually up at this time. Did she sense Jo's absence tonight?

Quietly, Jo got up, slipped on her trainers and sweater and tiptoed out to the back porch. Sitting on the top step, she used her cell to phone the duty nurse. Yes, Nan had been up and restless but she'd settled back to sleep now. "This transition's often harder for the carer," the woman said kindly. "You'll find it easier as time goes on."

Jo assured her she was coping and rang off.

At this time of the morning, the air temperature had dropped to a crystalline cold. Clouds covered the moon and she could smell rain coming but Jo didn't go inside.

Instead she bowed over her clasped knees and started to cry. Silent painful sobs grew in intensity until her rib cage heaved with them, until they escaped in soft wet gasps that she tried to smother in the prickly wool of her sweater.

The porch light came on and the screen door banged. Sitting on the step beside her, Dan hauled her into his arms. She buried her face into his chest. "It's just so hard to let her go."

He'd thrown on jeans and a shirt before coming out but the shirt wasn't buttoned and her tears wet his naked torso. The muscles in his back shifted and bunched under her cold, clutching fingers.

Jo struggled to pull herself together and let him go, but she couldn't. Right now he was the only anchor she had. She cried and cried. "That's right," he encouraged. "Let it all out."

She was conscious of the texture of his skin, baby-smooth over taut pecs, male nipples tightened in the cold. He smelled of pine soap. The buckle of his belt dug into her hip...yet still Jo clung on. He stroked her hair with callused hands, rubbed her back and lulled her into believing that everything would be all right.

Oh, God, she had missed him so much, missed this unspoken understanding they had. And yet it was different, because he was half-naked, because he wanted to marry her—because even if she wanted to, she couldn't have him.

Her sobs abated to shuddering breaths. Sitting up, Jo dug in her jeans for a hanky and blew her nose. "I'm okay now." She wiped her face dry on her woolen sleeve. "I'm sorry, you must be freezing."

With his thumb, he caught a missed tear on the curve of her jaw. "I'll live."

"Here." Brusquely, Jo caught the edges of his shirt, intending to button them. Her palms brushed skin and she swallowed hard. Under the porch light, they stared at each other, the air charged with awareness. A second passed, two—then his mouth touched hers.

Wrapping her arms around his neck, she pulled him closer. One kiss, she pacified the dissenting voice inside her.

Dan broke the contact and trailed his warm lips across her face. Then his mouth returned to hers and his languor gave way to an urgency that infected her. One kiss followed another, each one a drug that whispered *one more…just one more*.

He hauled her onto his lap, his splayed hands

falling to her hips as if he couldn't get enough of her. His erection pressed against her thigh. She was hot now, aching for him. Jo nipped his bare shoulder. His shirt was half off; had she done that? No, they were only kissing.

Jo captured his mouth. As long as they were only kissing she didn't have to stop. So she ignored Dan's caress, ignored that she was stroking him back. Time seemed to slow down. Her heartbeat quickened. Gradually Jo became aware she was straddling Dan's hard thighs. If they were naked he'd be inside her.

His hand slid under the sweater, up over her rib cage, around to the clasp of her bra. Jo wrenched her mouth away. "No!" In her panic she threw herself back, half sliding, half falling down the steps. At the bottom, she pushed to her feet. "Dammit, is that all you think about!"

After a short shocked silence, Dan said, "Don't you dare pretend this was only my idea."

"I just wanted a friend's shoulder to cry on." Jo shoved her shirttails into her jeans. "But never miss an opportunity to follow your own agenda, right, Dan?"

"That's unfair."

It was unfair but Jo was past caring. She'd put so much hard work into resisting him…and now they were back to square one. No, dammit, this was his fault. "You know I'm vulnerable!"

"Yeah, okay…maybe I…it wasn't planned but I…" His voice trailed off. Raking a hand through his hair, Dan stared at her. "I've been kidding myself," he rasped. "I've been kidding myself this whole time."

She felt a heady rush of relief. "Hallelujah, he's come to his senses."

"I'm in love with you."

Jo froze. The words seemed to hang in the chill air. She pushed them away. "No, you're not."

He wasn't listening. "Was I always? Maybe…I mean.… Who the hell cares?" His attention came back to her, his expression awed and intense. He held out a hand and said huskily, "I love you, Jo." Once she'd dreamed a man would look at her like this. But not this man.

And it didn't matter that this was part of some transference thing Dan had going with his grieving process. It didn't matter that he couldn't possibly appreciate how much he was hurting her right now because she'd never told him why all the things she'd wanted were out of her reach.

She'd come to the end of her emotional reserves and she would say anything to protect herself.

"The only thing you've done since you've come home is make my life harder. And I'm so *tired* of it, Dan." He paled, dropped his hand. "I don't *care* how much you think you need this to make sense of Lee and Steve's deaths, I don't love you beyond friendship, and I never will. Do you hear me!"

"I hear you." Under the porch light his face was expressionless. And in that vacuum, Jo heard her own heart. Oh, God, no. No! She took an involuntary step back.

She couldn't look at Dan and see the guy she should have had kids with…couldn't care about this stuff again.

Spinning on her heel, Jo half ran to her car. Dan didn't follow, didn't even call out. Her hands trembled so much she could barely wrench open the driver's door. The keys were in the ignition.

She started the engine and switched on the headlights, then remembered…her handbag was still inside. Jo clenched the steering wheel. She couldn't go back for it.

There was a tap on her window. Dan stood there holding her bag, the feminine accessory incongruous against his muscled torso. He still hadn't done up his shirt.

Averting her face, Jo opened the door, fumbled for the handbag, then shut the door. Neither

of them had said a word. Her car jolted down the
rough track toward the main road. By the time
she'd reached home she'd shut down thought,
feeling, emotion.

CHAPTER ELEVEN

JO WOKE THE NEXT morning desperate to salvage something out of last night's slash and burn. But first she needed to breakfast with Nan and catch up on her workload at the *Chronicle*. That included scheduling a final meeting with CommLink. Even that couldn't cheer her up. She jumped every time her office phone rang but it was never the call she wanted and Dan didn't return the messages she left him.

By the time she finally pulled up at the farmhouse it was close to five and her nerves were shot. Dan was a distant silhouette, working on the west ridge. He would have seen her car arriving so Jo waited. Five minutes passed, ten and he made no move to come down.

Well, what did she expect?

Swapping her shoes for the smallest pair of gum boots on the porch, Jo started climbing in as direct a line as the electric fences allowed. A mob of glossy black bulls with massive shoulders, skinny rumps and surly expressions tracked her progress.

"He'll forgive me," she told them. *He has to.*

The weather had been moody all day, trying on all four seasons like a teenage girl who couldn't decide what to wear. As she climbed the wind picked up, chilling as the sun began to dip behind the horizon. Belatedly Jo remembered she'd left her jacket in the car, but her heels were already starting to burn in the oversized boots so she pushed on.

Dan was bent over a concrete water trough, his arms immersed to the elbow. Splashes of mud and water stained his old gray T-shirt and jeans. When she was within a hundred yards, he straighened. Putting down the dripping pliers, he dried his arms on a rag from the toolbox on the back of the ATV and waited, arms folded. Jo swallowed. He had his soldier face on. Granite. Impassive. Suddenly the bulls didn't look as menacing.

Her heel was burning like a live coal but Jo refused to limp. She wasn't going for the pity vote. Still, she was pathetically grateful when the dogs came running to welcome her, all hot breath and wagging tails. Pausing to pat them, she called casually, "You're putting in long hours."

"There's a lot to do."

Jo noticed her hands were trembling and stuck

them into the pocket of her trousers. "Well, you're more than capable."

He stared at her, incredulous, before returning to his work.

Taking a deep breath Jo closed the last few yards. Cattle had churned the overflow around the trough into thick mud; Dan's gum boots were caked with it. She stopped on dry ground. "I guess you know why I'm here."

"Yeah." Reaching into the trough with one hand he pulled out a circular valve and inspected it. "You've come to apologize for telling the truth."

"And to confess to a lie," she said.

He glanced up.

"I denied feeling a sexual attraction because I wanted to reinforce my argument that we shouldn't get married."

Dan swished the valve clean.

Jo persevered. "So when I found myself climbing all over you when we're very close to getting our old relationship back. Well, I overreacted and I'm sorry." She caught the float, cupping it like a crystal ball. The underside of the black plastic sphere was covered in algae, soft like silk. The icy water numbed her fingers. "Then when you said you…" Her throat closed on the words. She tried again. "You don't, you know… Love me." She managed a laugh. "Heck, after my behavior last night you've probably already realized that. Lucky escape, right?"

He stuck his hand in the water. The round float on the surface bobbed on the ripples. "Can you hand me that pair of multigrips?"

Jo wiped her hands on her suit pants, her fingers so cold they ached, then squelched through the mud to get them. "I mean, c'mon," she joked. "We both know I've always been a nut job when it comes to romance."

Dan accepted the pliers, thrust both hands in the trough and seemed to be tightening something. "Are you done?"

"Done?" she said nervously.

He took the float and refastened it to the valve with twine. "Is it my turn?"

She dug her hands in her pockets. "Sure."

Straightening, he folded his arms. "First off, don't tell me how I feel. This isn't some knee-jerk grief reaction to Lee and Steve's death." His eyes blazed. "Secondly, don't patronize me, or, worse, try and save my ego by blaming your kooky history. We've been friends too long to start bullshitting each other now. If nothing else we've got honesty."

Jo bit her lip. "Okay."

"I love you," he said. "Deal with it. Last night you said you could never feel the same way. Is that still true?"

Jo dropped her gaze to the muddy gum boots. "I'm sorry," she said because that wasn't a lie. There was a moment's silence.

"I'll cancel the wedding," said Dan.

She looked up but his expression was unreadable.

The wind cut through her business shirt and Jo shivered. "I'd hate to lose your friendship over this."

"You won't." Picking up the tools, he carried them over to the ATV. "I'll give you a ride back if you don't mind sharing with Blue. The younger dogs can run."

She wanted to say something, anything to dissolve the tension, but her mind was a miserable blank.

"Here, put this on." Dan untied his bush jacket from around his waist and tossed it to her.

"Aren't you cold?"

"I'm used to it." While he cleared room for her in the ATV's tray, she pulled the green-and-black checked Swanndri over her head. It was still warm and the thick-weave wool smelled of earth and rain, of diesel and Dan. Tears pricked her eyes. Blue jumped up beside her, and she put an arm around him. Straddling the farm bike, Dan started the engine. Now there wasn't an opportunity for conversation, even if she could think of something to say.

Halfway down the track, he stopped and idled the engine. "Mind opening the gate?"

She scrambled off, ignoring her blister, eager to assist him. Dan drove through and glanced back, catching her anxious expression as Jo closed the gate. He smiled, the same smile parents used after they'd told their kids that mommy and daddy are getting a divorce but nothing will change. Promise.

The rest of the journey passed torturously slow. Jo watched the sunset leach color from the surrounding landscape and splash the clouds in increasingly violent shades of pink and red, purple and orange and told herself they'd get past this. In a few weeks, a few months at the outside Dan would get over her and they'd go back to the way things were.

He stopped the ATV beside her car. "Here you go."

Releasing Blue, Jo climbed down reluctantly, then took off Dan's Swanndri and handed it to him. "I need my shoes."

"I'll get them." He gave her another forced smile and her misery increased. Who was she kidding? Nothing would ever be the same.

She watched as he walked to the porch. The motion-detector light triggered, revealing Dan's features as he picked up her shoes. Her throat ached. *Please don't hurt this much. I'm trying to protect you.*

Returning, he held out the shoes. "It was never my intention to make your life harder, Jo."

She stared at them. *If nothing else, we've got honesty.* "I had cancer," she said in a choked voice.

Dan froze. "What?"

"It wasn't a shoulder injury that had me in the hospital when you visited—I'd had a mastectomy." His shocked gaze dropped to her breasts and she resisted the urge to cross her arms. "The left. I'm wearing a prosthesis."

Dan opened his mouth, closed it.

"My prognosis looks good." Her tone brisk, Jo kicked off the oversized gum boots. Facts, not feelings. "The lymph nodes weren't affected and they caught it early but I'm still twelve and a half months away from the first watershed, let alone the magical five-year mark."

"This is why you pushed me away last night?" His voice was hoarse

Jo inspected her left heel, saw blood and slipped on her shoes anyway. "In a substantial percentage, breast cancer recurs up to twelve years later, even in low-risk patients like me."

"Is that why you've given up on marriage and kids?"

Picking up the gum boots, she held them out. "One study I read said even with adjuvant therapy—chemo or radiation—for more than twenty percent of node-negative patients, their disease recurred within fifteen years after diagnosis."

Dan automatically accepted the gum boots. "Why didn't you tell me when you were diagnosed…or at the bar? I'm your best friend, dammit!"

"I was still hoping for the best. The next time I saw you was ten days after surgery when you returned for the funerals. You didn't need any more bad news."

The porch light flicked off; impatiently he activated it again, his brain putting all the pieces together. The immobile arm that stopped her from hugging him when he'd visited her in hospital—not the result of shoulder surgery. The bar… Jo only got drunk when she was in trouble. Her desperation when she'd made a pass.

"The night in Auckland when you were trying to pick up guys?"

"Surgery had been scheduled the next day and I wanted a last fling in case…" Jo shrugged and checked her shoe again. "Except the med-student bartender was right. I couldn't have surgery with alcohol in my system. Between work and Nan it was five weeks before I went under the knife."

He was still processing her first sentence. "You wanted a last fling in case you lost a breast." With sickening force it hit him that he'd scared away her last prospect then rejected her. "Does Nan know?"

She shook her head. "No one knows except Polly. She was my nurse at Auckland Hospital, semi-retired and looking for a change of scene after her divorce. Initially, I hired her for postoperative care and to help out part-time while I was having chemo. We told Nan she was a housekeeper. And then as my condition improved and Nan's deteriorated, she simply swapped patients."

"What about work?"

"I went to Auckland for chemo last thing Friday, recovered over the weekend and was back at work in Beacon Bay on Monday. When the side effects kicked in, I either worked from home or I delegated. Everyone assumed my absence had something to do with Nan's worsening dementia."

Dan realized he was still holding the gum boots and dropped them. "You kept this to yourself, dealt with it all by yourself? Why?"

"Because I didn't want people looking at me the way you are now," she said sharply.

"I needed things to stay normal. It was hard enough dealing with cancer myself without…" Again, she stopped.

"Without seeing your fear reflected in other people's eyes?" He closed his own, suddenly understanding her rationale for not telling him the truth. Dan wanted to shake her; he wanted to hold her. He wanted to cry for everything she'd suffered alone.

He stripped his expression, grateful for the discipline of years of training. "So you're denying yourself a chance to love because of a twenty percent chance of recurrence." Later he'd deal with his own fears of that; right now he had a future to fight for.

"That's after five years, remember. And it's not just about recurrence." Jo swallowed. "Chemo may have affected my fertility and I know you eventually want kids."

He took a step toward her. "I want you more."

She backed away. "Even if I could conceive, I don't know if I want to have children with this hanging over me.… It wouldn't be fair."

"Fair. Since when is life fair?" The porch light went off. He pulled off one work boot and threw it at the motion sensor. The light flicked back on. "Don't you know I'm here for you no matter what?"

But she was already shaking her head. "I won't let you make that sacrifice."

"It's not a sacrifice, it's a choice and I've made it." Again Dan closed the gap. "I choose you."

"Stop and think about this, Dan," she challenged him. "You really want to marry a woman who might die? You've already lost Steve and Lee this year. You think I don't see how much you're suffering? It's eating you up."

"All the more reason to make every day count."

"No." Turning, Jo strode back to her vehicle. "I'm not dragging you into my waiting game."

Wearing one work boot, Dan followed her. "What you're really saying is that I don't have the cojones to marry a woman living with cancer."

That stopped her. Their eyes locked. In the near dark he couldn't make out her expression. "Nice try," she said and opened the car door.

"I didn't get the chance to fight alongside them," he said quietly. "Don't deny me the chance to fight alongside you."

Jo leaned her forehead on the edge of the open door. Dan waited. The interior car light illuminated her face as she turned, using the door as a barrier. "I'll accept your support, but only as a friend."

Dan remembered her expression last night when he'd told her he loved her. He would never let her shut him out again.

Pulling the door out of her hands, he backed her against the car, holding her there with his body. "I love you," he said. "That's nonnegotiable. How do you feel about me?"

"Under the circumstances, having a relationship would be selfish and irrespon—"

He kissed her. With so much yearning, so much need and persuasion that she had no choice but to kiss him back. With a groan, Jo wrenched her mouth away.

"The fear's always going to be there," she warned.

"In the SAS they teach you that it's how you dance with it that makes the difference."

She closed her eyes.

Sliding one hand behind her nape, Dan nuzzled her neck. "Dance with me," he murmured against her skin, felt her responsive shiver.

"I don't—"

He kissed her again, taking his time, doing it right. "Yes," he insisted. "You do." He saw with satisfaction that, cheeks flushed and heavy-lidded, she wasn't thinking very clearly anymore.

"Damn you," she said then kissed him without reservations.

"We need to talk about how this is going to work," she managed when they broke apart.

"Later." Tugging her into the house, he pushed open the door to his bedroom. "First I owe you a night."

CHAPTER TWELVE

JO GRABBED THE DOORJAMB. "Dan, I'm not ready."

"You'll never be ready." Shifting his hold, he gently pried her hand free and turned on the light. "And the longer we leave this, the harder it will be for you."

Anger threaded through her panic. "You asshole, I need you to be sensitive about this."

He sat on the bed, holding her easily on his lap. "Tell me this," he said, "if I had testicular cancer and lost one of my balls would it make a difference in your wanting me?"

"No, but this is different."

"Why, because a breast is bigger? Okay, what if I'd lost an arm or a leg.… I'm trying to figure out, Jo, which missing body part would make me unlovable."

She laughed, half in despair. "It's not about love, it's about desire. You've always been a breast man." She'd postponed reconstructive surgery in favor of making the quickest recovery possible. At the time she hadn't seen sex in her immediate future, let alone falling for her best friend.

He tucked a loose curl behind her ear. "One will do."

"I can't believe you're trying to make a joke out of this." She scrambled off his lap. "You know this is difficult."

"Yeah, but we're not going to make it tragic." He held out his hand. "Nothing could stop you being the sexiest woman on the planet to me, Jo," he said. "Nothing."

Her heart was so high in her throat she could hardly breathe but she took his hand. He was right. Sooner or later they had to deal with this. Lightly, he drew her down beside him. "Show me."

Jo hesitated, then, fingers trembling, she undid her shirt and shrugged it off. Reaching for the snap, her courage deserted her. It had taken her a long time to make peace with her lopsided chest, to look in the mirror without flinching. "I can't...please. At least let our first time be with the bra on."

Instantly, she was engulfed in his comforting arms. "If that's you want."

What she wanted was her breast back. Even if it didn't matter to Dan, it mattered to her. *Deal with it*.

Feeling ugly, unsexy and sad, Jo tried to

relax into Dan's embrace. She nestled against his body, hard with muscle. He was so beautiful, this man…perfect.

And though she was no longer perfect, she let the hot, insistent pressure of his mouth cloud her mind with lust until she could pretend they were back in her Auckland hotel room.

There was no doubt he wanted her, the denim straining over his erection proved that. His rippled abdomen tightened when she unzipped his jeans, slid her hand lower. His cock was hard, and hot and smooth.

He hauled her closer, his lower body trapping her hand, and began his own exploration, unzipping her trousers, caressing her through her panties. "How many months I've wanted to do this," he rasped between long slow kisses while Jo moved restlessly under his skillful fingers. Yes, she wanted this, wanted him. But she would set the ground rules.

Jo rolled free. "Take off your clothes."

He chuckled. "If you do, too."

They kicked off their pants together and she helped him remove his shirt, comfortable in her prosthesis bra. It was full cupped with a pocket for a silicon insert, complete with nipple. He would never know the difference even by touching—except perhaps by comparing the warmth to her real flesh?

Jo stalled.

Dan slid down the bed, gently pressing her knees apart, shocking her into paying attention. Was he…?

She gasped as he licked her inner thigh, then moved higher, sending her arching off the bed, all nerve endings and sensation. And, as with everything he did, he was so wickedly competent she climaxed within minutes.

Slowly, Dan kissed his way up her body. She opened her mouth to protest weakly and he cut her off, his tongue demanding and passionate.

She had to take charge of this while she still could. Threading her hands through his thick hair, Jo tugged to make him shift his weight. Rolling him onto his back, she straddled him, pressing his fingers to her remaining breast, needing his touch.

Because she was a breast person, too.

Instinctively his other hand went to the prosthesis cup and she intercepted it, lacing their fingers together and hiding her sadness under lowered lashes. Then she smiled, because his erection was hard and hot against her.

Delaying the moment, she slid against him, tormenting them both. "Patience," she teased and he growled. She kissed that fierce mouth, nipping his lower lip, before sitting back. His fingers tightened on her breast. Every time she became aware of the covering bra, Jo remembered she was disfigured. This time Dan saw her frustration.

"Take the bra off, Jo."

"No." It shouldn't matter to her and yet it did. Angry, she climbed off him. *He's not the one repulsed, you are.* "Let's wait until I've had reconstructive surgery." Months, that meant months of sexual frustration. Why was she punishing herself? Punishing them?

He was watching her carefully. "Okay."

God, she hated sympathy. "Don't worry," she snapped. "I can give you blow jobs in the meantime."

He had her on her back so quickly she didn't have time to do more than give a startled yelp. "Yeah, because that's all this is about."

"You should have accepted my offer in Auckland—" her voice broke "—when I was perfect."

"I didn't love that Jo," he said gently, "I love *this* one. And I don't care about perfect. I just care that you're here." She pressed her palms against his chest, and he moved to let her sit up. Without giving herself time to think, Jo unfastened her bra and pulled it off. Fighting the urge to close her eyes, she watched as Dan's gaze went to her scar, a ten-centimeter line across where her left breast should have been.

Just over a year after surgery, it was still a welt of angry red, in and of itself nothing to shock the squeamish. It was the position that unsettled Jo. Instead of a curve there was flatness, no nipple. Beside it, the lushness of her right breast only seemed to highlight the oddness, the sense of something missing.

Dan's chest expanded in a silent, careful breath and Jo died inside. Impossible not to notice his erection had subsided, not fully enough to make her feel…ugly. Rejected.

"I should have been there for you," he said, his voice ragged.

She'd never thought that he might feel excluded. Jo pulled him close and buried her face in his neck. The muscles were corded, tense. "I'm sorry," she whispered, pressing her lips against them. "Dan, I'm sorry. I did what I thought was best at the time."

Grabbing her shoulders, he forced her back. "Don't you ever shut me out again, you hear me?" He was crying. She had never seen him cry.

Shocked, Jo shook her head.

"Promise me!"

"I promise."

He dropped his hands. One cupped her right breast, the other traced the scar. The pad of his thumb moved gently over the puckered flesh.

Because tears rolled down his cheeks, Jo suffered the touch. But when he lowered his head to kiss her there she pushed him away. Dan caught her hands and laid his lips to her surgical scar. "Don't you know war wounds are a badge of pride?" he said gruffly. "Besides, this one's a baby."

Of course, he'd seen worse. There was no shock. Still, she was horrified, watching him touch it. On a practical level she might have made peace with her physical loss but not her loss of sensuality. What was a woman's femininity without her breasts?

"What do you feel when I do this?" he asked. Only traces of tears remained on his lean cheeks.

"I'm still numb." *Inside and out.*

"Will you feel more with reconstruction?"

"No." Her throat hurt. "All the benefits are psychological."

He stroked the scar again. "You know what *I* feel?"

"Horror?" She couldn't quite make that a joke. "Compassion?" Almost worse.

He spread his fingers wide over the scar, over her heart. "Gratitude. If it wasn't for this, you might not be here."

"See," she said, blinking hard. "You're being kind. But kind isn't sexy, is it?"

"You want sexy, Jo?" His voice grew husky, and she noticed he'd become hard again. Lifting her gaze to his, her stomach dropped. Naked, Dan rose from the bed and went to the closet, his movements strong and graceful. Tanned everywhere but his buttocks. He opened the wardrobe door wide and she saw a reflection of the bed, then her surprised face.

"God bless Mom's vanity," he said. "Full-length mirrors everywhere." He sat on the edge of the bed and positioned her between his legs so they were both facing the mirror. Jo stared at the scar cutting across the right side of her chest and her excitement dissipated. She focused on Dan instead.

His body was a warm wall behind her, his erection solid against the small of her back. Strong male legs, bracketed her smooth, pale ones; his shoulders and biceps dwarfed hers. In comparison she looked fragile, pale and utterly feminine.

Except for that scar.

He trailed her neck with lazy nibbles and the woman in the mirror grew heavy-lidded. Her remaining breast with its peaked nipple lifted as she tangled her fingers in his tawny hair and tilted her head to give him better access.

Dan lifted his head; over her shoulder his eyes burned. She remembered that intent look from when he'd come to her house with the lillies…like she was prey and he was a hunter. Jo swallowed and gripped his iron-hard thighs.

"You're so beautiful," he whispered, his breath sending a shiver down her spine. "I knew you'd be beautiful naked."

One callused hand cupped her pale breast, the thumb circling and sensitizing the pink nipple. The other moved delicately over the scar, fanning out to cover her heart. The contrast in sensations made her squirm.

"You like that?"

"What else you got?" she panted.

With a chuckle, Dan spread her legs with those strong hands.

"Oh," Jo said weakly.

"Like you said up by the trough," he teased, starting another conversation with his fingers, "I'm more than capable." Minutes passed. In a darker tone, he said, "Feeling sexy yet?"

Jo watched herself writhe in the mirror. "That woman is a total slut," she managed. With an effort of will, she turned in his arms and pushed him down on the bed. "You're not going to have this all your own way, mister."

Dan spread his arms wide in surrender. His voice was as smoky as his eyes. "Don't you know I'm all yours yet?"

Her vision blurred and she blinked. She

wanted every second of this to be sharp and clear. She eased herself onto him.

For an infinite moment they paused like that, gazes locked, bodies joined. Outside a defiant warbler trilled a rising crescendo of notes… the sound like joy skipping and tripping over itself.

Then one of them moved, and every sound faded.

And Jo discovered some things could be perfect after all.

CHAPTER THIRTEEN

DEEPLY ASLEEP, Jo rolled onto her side, taking the blankets with her. It wasn't the first time. Smiling, Dan tugged at the blankets until she rolled back with a murmured protest, settling against his chest like she belonged there.

It felt good. It felt right.

All his life Dan had resisted the passionate, lifelong kind of love because his parents made it look like hard labor. Maybe that's why he'd been blind to Jo as more than a friend. Still, his bride needed some serious training in sharing a bed. He figured fifty years should do it.

Cupping his hand over her hair, Dan steeled himself to consider the implications of her cancer. He still couldn't deal with the fact that she'd kept him out of her treatment, so he pushed it aside. Jo could still die. The thought didn't evoke any kind of visceral reaction. Why?

Because I don't believe it.

And it wasn't just because she lay soft and warm in his arms and he felt more optimistic than he had for the first time in months.

Whether the cancer came back or not, Jo was a fighter. And to his last breath, Dan would fight alongside her.

"Your heartbeat has sped up," Jo said softly. "It woke me up."

"Go back to sleep."

"What were you thinking about?"

She knew. He could tell by the way her body had tensed.

"That we've just given this memory foam mattress something to remember."

He felt her smile against his heart. "I don't think that's how they work."

"You're right, it probably takes a few times to imprint." She gave a cry of surprise as he flipped her off him and rolled on top. "Better get onto that...."

THE PHONE RINGING DRAGGED Dan to consciousness. For a moment he blinked in the late-morning light. What the hell was he doing in bed so late? Then he remembered.

Over the sound of the phone, he could hear the shower running in the bathroom down the hall. Smiling, he rolled over the indent from her body to reach for the phone. "Isn't life wonderful?" he greeted his caller.

"Dan...hi," said his cousin's widow.

Pulling up the sheet, Dan swung his feet to

the floor. "Claire." He cursed himself for his insensitivity. "I've been meaning to phone and check on you and Lewis."

"Hey, I can just as easily phone you." Except she never did. "Anyway, I'm RSVPing to your wedding invitation."

"Look, I understand if you don't want to come—"

"Don't be silly, we wouldn't miss it for the world." Her tone rang too bright. "Steve and I always thought you and Jo belonged together... but you guys could never see it."

He scratched his head. "Why didn't you ever say anything?"

"Because you both would have run a mile."

Dan chuckled. "It'll be good to see you," he said gruffly.

"I'm looking forward to catching up with everyone." She hesitated. "So who's the best man, Ross or Nate?"

The familiar band of grief tightened around Dan's chest. They both knew who it should have been. "Ross. Nate can't make it back."

"You're kidding, right?"

Dan understood Claire's shock. A former foster kid, Nate had adopted his SAS brothers as his own. He was the one who organized social get-togethers and remembered birthdays. Hell, he even made them celebrate the anniversary of their first deployment as a troop. This year it had come and gone unmarked.

"I guess we just have to give him some time," she said.

If time could really heal. Nate had been the last man standing, fighting alone to defend his wounded and dead comrades. Dan's jaw ached; he unclenched his teeth. He had no right to suffer like this—not compared to Nate or Ross, not compared to Claire and Lewis or Lee's bereaved family and fiancée, Julia.

"So I talked to Jules yesterday." Claire seemed to read his mind. "She didn't know about the wedding."

"Until yesterday I wasn't sure if Jo would have me." He tried not to sound defensive. "Jules and Lee were supposed to be getting married last month…would she even want an invitation?"

"She'd want to be asked. Even if she doesn't feel up to coming. And sometimes it can help being around other people who love and miss—" Her voice wobbled. "Hang on a second?"

Dan had been hungry when he'd woken up, ravenous after a night's lovemaking. Now his stomach knotted. Claire had once been his roommate; he'd introduced her and Steve. Yet he had to fight the urge to hang up on her because there was nothing he could do to take her pain away. *I should have been there.*

"Sorry," she said, coming back on the line. "False alarm. I thought someone was at the door."

He didn't challenge the lie. "Is Lewis okay? Mom said you've been having a few problems."

"We're working through it."

"If there's anything you need—"

"You'll be the first person I call. Listen, I've gotta go. Give Jo my love and see you both soon." The forced cheerfulness was back in her voice. Dan knew with a sinking feeling that when she hung up she'd cry.

"Claire, wait.... Come a few days early. It's duck-shooting season. I promised Lewis I'd take him out this year." They'd both promised, he and Steve.

"He'd like that," she said awkwardly. "Thanks, Dan."

It's the least I can do. He said goodbye, hung up and stared at the pile of clothes on the chair.

With a groan, he buried his face in his hands. "Dammit, I should have been there!"

He felt a touch on his bare shoulder. "Dan?"

Turning, he pulled Jo onto the bed, and kissed her like his life depended on it.

"Wow," she said when they broke apart.

She'd dressed in the jeans and sweater she'd worn yesterday, dark red hair, still damp from the shower, feathered her forehead. "If I didn't have a date with Nan, I'd demand an encore." Though she was smiling, she searched his face. "Are you okay? I heard—"

"That was Claire." Dan rolled to his feet, then pulled Jo up. "She and Lewis can make the wedding." Naked, he padded into the bathroom and turned on the shower.

Jo followed. "What wedding?"

"Very funny. You. Me. Twelve days' time… ring any wedding bells?" He adjusted the water temperature. "Ouch, maybe we should both lay off the morning jokes."

Stepping into the shower, he lifted his face to the spray.

Jo reached in and turned off the water. "You said you'd cancel."

Baffled, Dan reached for a towel, wiped his face dry, then draped it around his waist and got out. "Didn't we clear this up last night? I love you, you love me. We're back in business."

"You talked me into a relationship, Dan, not marriage."

He stared at her. "We agreed you wouldn't shut me out again."

"And I'm not. If I'm cancer-free in another two years, if my fertility's unaffected and if you're still in love with me—" she smiled at him "—then we'll definitely talk about it."

She turned on the shower again. Dan turned it off. "And if there's a recurrence or your fertility has been compromised, then what? You'll cut me loose?"

"I don't know what I'll do," she said candidly. "I only know I love you too much to let you burn any bridges now."

Her admission of love eased him. "Idiot." On a wave of tenderness Dan lifted her into a bear hug, the wool of her sweater soft against his wet chest. "What kind of man would I be to wait until you can offer me some kind of guarantee?"

Her arms went around his neck in a mock stranglehold. "What kind of woman would I be if I dragged you along on the scariest part of the ride?"

He gave her a little shake. "Trust us...trust *me*."

She shook her head. "It's not a question of trust—"

"You love me but you're not going to rely on me?" Dan put her down and folded his arms. "It sure as hell feels like a trust issue to me."

Jo glared back at him. "It's plain common sense."

"Postponing our lives out of lack of courage

isn't how either of us has lived and we're not starting now. The wedding stands."

Her jaw set. "Call me later—when you can talk sense about this."

"Talking solves nothing, only action." Calmly, he went back in the shower, turned it on. "We're getting married."

Jo said nothing, but shoved the dial to cold.

"Temper, temper." Reaching for the soap, Dan began washing.

"If you won't protect yourself, I will." Through the shower curtain he watched her leave, her exasperated flounce accentuating the swing of her hips.

The water was still cold. Slowly he turned it back to hot, feeling the sting of it on his chilled skin. But the heat didn't penetrate deeply.

He should have been there when she faced surgery and Nan's health started failing.

And he wasn't.

Dan had to get her to the altar because he couldn't let that happen again.

Jo drove to Pinehill high on love and simultaneously itching to wring the object of her affection's neck.

Dan was going to be stubborn about this. He'd had what she called his Terminator face on—calm but lethally focused. Last night she'd thought they'd reached an understanding. If she could go back to the moment by her car, that fatal hesitation, then…

Honesty compelled her to admit she wouldn't have done it any differently. It was damned inconvenient and the worst timing ever but she loved Dan and all she could do now was try to minimize the damage. Maybe she couldn't safeguard her own future, but she could safeguard his.

Reaching for her cell, she rang Anton at the bar but he only repeated what he'd told her the first time she tried to cancel the reception. "My contract's with Dan, Jo, not you. He said if it's not a wedding, it's a wake… Incidentally he rang a few minutes ago with a message."

Of course Dan knew she'd do this. "What is it?"

"He loves you."

Damn him, damn him, damn him. "Thanks, Anton."

Next she phoned Father O'Malley, who'd known them both since childhood. He listened with characteristic sympathy. "Obviously I've made it very clear that I won't perform the service if you're unwilling but he said he'd take that risk. You know Dan."

Oh, yes, she knew Dan.

"He left a message for you."

"I know," Jo said grimly. "He loves me."

"No, keep dinner free. He wants to take you dancing…good at it, apparently."

She hung up and tossed the cell onto the passenger seat. Why couldn't Dan understand her need to protect him? Getting married required the kind of faith she'd lost when she'd woken up without a breast. When her odds of survival improved, when she'd got better at living with the possibility of recurrence, *then* they could discuss commitment.

At Pinehill, she found Nan in the dining room clearing breakfast plates to vociferous complaints from those residents still eating. "It's past eight," Rosemary protested. "We need to get crops planted to feed our brave boys."

She was obviously back in her WWII land girl years.

"Very true, Rosemary," said the nurse. "But rest your arm first. You need to be fighting fit, too."

"Yes, I'd better sit down a minute. Perhaps you'd like to take over." She caught sight of Jo, who waited patiently while she shifted gears. "Jocelyn, you're not a land girl."

"No, love. I'm here to take you to the garden center." Nan wasn't the only resident bemoaning the lack of a vegetable garden, and yesterday

Jo had offered to buy plants for a small strip of bare earth outside the kitchen window.

"I don't know…" Nan was obviously torn. "I'm needed here."

The nurse returning plates to the diners said amiably, "We'll manage for an hour and you'll find the best deals."

"That's true." All business, Nan turned back to Jo. "Where's my purse?" They went to Nan's room and collected it, along with her coat. "Do you know," she confided on the way to the car, "what the secret is to setting jam?"

"No, tell me."

"Methylated spirit." Nan chuckled.

"You're kidding!"

"The pips are full of pectin. If you soak them overnight you can use the water next day as a setting agent." Nan burbled on and Jo devoted herself to showing her grandmother a good time, buying twice the number of plants they needed once they reached the nursery.

An hour later, she'd settled Nan in the car and was loading plants into the trunk when a middle-aged blonde came out of the hairdressers' opposite and hailed her. For a moment Jo didn't recognize her.

"Pat?"

"Yes, it's me." Dan's mother crossed the parking lot, flicking her platinum bob out of her eyes. "I've just had it colored." She struck a pose. "What do you think?"

"Very chic," Jo reassured her.

"I talked to Dan this morning, he mentioned you stayed over last night."

Jo had a sudden vivid recollection of how they'd employed Pat's old mirror and blushed. The older woman eyed the color in her cheeks. "Does this mean you've changed your mind about marrying him?"

"No, it's too soon to be thinking about commitment."

"I'm glad," said Pat, then added hastily, "only because we can't be sure whether grief is still influencing his actions."

Jo remembered his anguish after Claire's phone call—*I should have been there*—and the desperation in his kiss. Feeling sick, she looked at Pat. "Maybe it's also influencing his feelings for me?"

"No." Pat shook her head. "Dan is like his father, a one-woman man." Jo couldn't hide her relief or her surprise, and Pat smiled. "There are worse things than having you as a daughter-in-law." She sounded wistful.

Jo finished loading the plants and closed the trunk. "I was sorry to hear about you and Herman."

"Don't be. Europe will be much more fun

with a girlfriend." Under the perfect makeup, Pat's face was drawn and sad. "Maybe I'll add New York and stay a couple months with my prodigal daughter."

"What's taking so long?" Nan called.

"Is that your grandmother? I must say hello." Pat opened the passenger door. "Rosemary, long time no see."

Nan smiled uncertainly.

"It's me, Pat. You might not recognize me because I've had my hair dyed blond."

"You mean you chose that color?"

Pat's smile faded.

Jo moved in quickly for damage control. "You know Dan's mother," she prompted.

"Such a nice boy, Daniel," exclaimed Nan. "I was always surprised how well he turned out considering his mother."

Bewildered, Pat looked at Jo.

"Nan, this *is*—"

"I've always said that woman would much happier if she stopped blaming her husband for everything that's wrong with her life—oh, are we at the garden center already?" Looking beyond a dumbstruck Pat, Nan started fidgeting with her seat belt. "Help me unbuckle this."

Nudging Pat aside, Jo retrieved one of the plants and showed it to Nan. "We've already picked up some lovely vegetable seedlings, see? And now we're leaving."

Rosemary took the plant and settled back in her seat. "Well, get a wriggle on, they'll need watering."

Jo shut the car door and turned to Pat. "I'm so sorry," she murmured. "She doesn't realize what she's saying most of the time."

"Forget about it." Pat tried to smile. On impulse Jo hugged her. She looked as though she really needed a hug.

"It's not true, you know." Pat's voice was as small and plaintive as a little girl's. "If I wasn't taking responsibility I wouldn't have asked for a divorce."

"You can always change your mind."

Pat gave a choked little laugh. "Has Dan ever told you what Herman calls our granddaughter? Attila. And yet he's so terrified I'll change my mind he's prepared to spend a week in Auckland with her to avoid me."

"Jocelyn," Nan called impatiently, "what are we waiting for?"

"Coming." Jo looked at Pat. "If you need someone to talk to…"

"Oh, I have a hundred girlfriends, don't worry. Or I can phone one of my daughters. Nice to see you again, Rosemary," Pat called, then with a nod to Jo, walked back across the road, her platinum hair glinting like a helmet in the sun.

"Who was that?" Nan asked, when Jo got into the driver's seat.

"Someone I feel like I've met for the first time. Let me make a quick call." She keyed in Dan's number.

"Jo." Husky, sexy…and wary. He'd said her name a thousand times but this was the first she'd gone weak at the knees. Good thing she was sitting.

"Dan, I just saw your mother. I think she regrets asking for a divorce. Maybe you should tell your dad?"

There was a moment of silence. He'd expected another argument. "Hell, no. I learned my lesson. I'm staying out of it. Anyway, it's not as bad as Mom thinks. Meredith's having marital problems and Herman's sticking around for a few days to watch the kids while she and Charlie thrash it out. My sister doesn't want Mom charging in so we're keeping that quiet."

"But they had the perfect marriage," Jo said, stunned. "Well, Meredith is perfect," she amended. Dan's sister was gentle and sweet, the opposite of her bombastic husband.

"I like that you're already biased toward the Jansen side," he approved.

"At least phone your mother. I really think she needs moral support."

"Are we doing dinner?"

"Are you trying to blackmail me?" But Jo had already decided her best shot at talking him out of the wedding was to get together to do just that: talk.

"I prefer to think of it as lovemail," he teased and Jo began to understand why he always got his girl. "I'll pick you up at six."

As she rang off, Nan said, "Now how on earth did I do that?" She was gazing at her cast with a puzzled expression.

Jo braced herself. "You had a fall."

"Did I?" Nan might have forgotten, but Jo would always remember she'd let her own emotional needs take precedence over her grandmother's best interests. Never again would she allow her heart to overrule her head.

CHAPTER FOURTEEN

SWEAT TRICKLING DOWN her breastbone, Jo removed her cardigan and tried to concentrate on *Chronicle* paperwork. The late afternoon sun beat on her head making it difficult to concentrate. On a sunny autumn's day, Pops's glass-walled conservatory addition was a heat trap, but all the files she needed were stored in this room.

Vince Bugatti crooned in the background, alleviating the ache left by Nan's absence. She'd be glad when the house sold. It wasn't the same without her grandmother and anyway the money was needed for her care. Opening the monthly accounts book, Jo's mind drifted. She'd rent somewhere close to the sea. Dan would visit and they'd lie on the beach, soaking up rays like this....

On impulse she stripped off her long-sleeved T-shirt, felt the sun's caress on her skin. Lovely.

This past summer had mostly slipped by unnoticed. Nan wasn't a beach person. Jo shook her head at her pale arms and stomach, then caught sight of a faint redness near her navel. What..? She looked closer and smiled. Beard burn.

Yesterday she wouldn't have done this, but today she pulled off her top and sat in the sun in her bra. Leaning back in the armchair, Jo raised her arms above her head, welcoming the stretch in her shoulders and spine. Enjoying the return of her sensuality.

Where once she used to sleep naked, now she even wore a bra to bed under her nightdress. She'd become alienated from her own body. Jo looked down at the pretty lace hiding her disfigurement and took the bra off. Reclining the chair, she lay back with her eyes closed. The sun soaked into her bones, warming her torso without discrimination. Dan had kissed her scar.

Tentatively Jo stroked a hand over it. When the usual emotions came—distaste, horror, rejection—she replaced them with acceptance. This wasn't something she'd fix overnight, but if she tried…

Gently she touched her remaining breast, wanting to integrate it with the flat side, then swept both hands up and over the front of her torso.

Some sixth sense made Jo open her eyes. Dan

stood outside the conservatory. Instinctively she covered her nakedness. He didn't move, didn't react. He could have been a part of the landscape. Jo's panic subsided. She uncrossed her arms and returned her hands to her body. What had begun as exploratory became increasingly sexual. His eyes darkened.

Playfully, Jo rolled her nipple between her fingers, watched his ribs expand in a deep breath. It occurred to her she could use sex as a bargaining tool in the wedding argument, but she instantly dismissed it. She wouldn't sully this with politics.

Her other hand slid down her belly to the snap on her jeans. One button, two. Dan's eyes went to the triangle of white lace revealed, then lifted with a heat that sucked all the oxygen out of her lungs. Standing up, Jo discovered her legs were unsteady. She stepped forward and unlocked the conservatory ranch slider, then turned and walked upstairs to her bedroom. Dan followed. Neither of them spoke.

Jo lay down on the lurid green cover of her virginal single bed. "Hurry," she said.

DAN DIDN'T NEED TELLING twice. He hauled off Jo's jeans and panties, fumbled with his zip and freed himself enough to lie between those sweet legs. He'd give Jo what they both craved.

Only when he was inside her, only when she was wrapped around him, did he finally get enough control to stop and think about slowing this down.

He was still more or less fully clothed and Jo was naked under him. She was breathing as hard as he was, that little gasping pant that had him moving again before he was aware of it.

He was an hour and a half early for their dinner date, had puzzled the dogs by feeding them midafternoon and done the absolute minimum in terms of work. But he was in love for the first time in his life and incapable of staying away. He'd arrived with some idea of wooing her into marriage—women loved that stuff—but the moment he saw her, half-naked in the sun getting reacquainted with her body, he'd wanted her.

Good thing she wanted him.

The sex was hard and fast and furious and when they were done, the lime-green bedcover was on the floor. So were all the pillows. One hand holding Jo, Dan groped for a blanket and covered their bare asses. Jo chuckled. "You still have your shoes on."

What do you know? He did. "And they're hanging off the bed. How do you sleep in this thing?"

"When I move I'll buy a new one."

"You won't need to," he reminded her. "You'll be sleeping in mine."

"Sometimes I will, sometimes I'll be in my own bed."

"Are you deliberately trying to piss me off?"

Jo sat up, pulling the blanket around her shoulders. "Getting angry isn't going to change my mind about marrying you."

Dan pulled her back to his chest. "Then tell me what will."

"Nothing," she said firmly. But he didn't believe her. There had to be something. She was right in one thing, though. Anger wouldn't get him anywhere.

"We'll work this out," he said, because women like to hear a guy being reasonable. Jo gave him a squeeze of approval.

"I saw Mom today," he said, wanting another one. Pathetic. Love was making him pathetic. "You should have warned me about her hair."

"I hope you told her you liked it."

"Even Blue barked at her."

"Dan!" But he felt her silent laughter against his body. One of her feathery curls tickled his chin; he wrapped it around his index finger. "You didn't cut your hair to this length, did you?" he said quietly.

"No. I wore a wig when it started falling out

during chemo, then when it grew back enough, appeared with a radical new style. It came back wavy though. Chemo does that sometimes."

"I like it." Gently, Dan kissed the soft, baby-fine strands, but he was unsettled.

Jo stirred. "We need to talk about canceling the wedding."

"No. We'll only argue again." Getting up, he straightened his clothing and pulled up the zip on his jeans. "Here's an idea. Let's give ourselves some breathing space for a week. Enjoy this. Then we'll review."

"Meanwhile you'll carry on organizing the wedding," she said drily. "I don't think so."

He sat on the bed. "I promise I won't do a single thing on the wedding. It all stops."

"All right," she said. "But only if I get ten minutes a day—no interruptions—to argue my case for cancellation."

"We both do."

She sighed. "Fine."

"Our days are too busy to spend any real time together." He picked a dress out of her wardrobe, one he'd always liked. "I'm thinking nights."

"Sleepovers?" The way she said it made him want to get naked again.

"With Herman away, they'll have to be at the farm." When she looked suspicious he said patiently, "Jo, you have a single mattress."

She still wavered.

"Tell you what," he said. "I'll forgo my ten minutes' talking for it." He'd do his persuading in bed. *Their* bed.

"Give me your ten minutes and we have a deal."

She really thought she had a shot at talking him out of this. He tried not to be offended.

"Tough negotiator," he said bitterly.

"You know the saying…all's fair in love and war."

"Glad we understand each other."

"Dan," she dropped the sheet and came over, soft, naked and vulnerable. "You will keep an open mind about this, won't you?"

"If you will," he said and watched his soft, naked and vulnerable bride look away.

"Of course." She kissed him. He kissed his little Judas back.

"And you won't go organizing the wedding behind my back, will you?"

"I promise," he said.

There was nothing left to do.

"I AM PICKING UP a hottie tonight." Her red dress swirling around her sturdy calves, Delwyn shimmied off the dimly lit dance floor and wiggled into the booth next to Jo, smelling of peach schnapps and Anaïs Anaïs.

Gulping at her cocktail, she flicked back her long dark hair, fired a lopsided wink at a group of guys at the bar and repeated her new mantra, "Being single is the bes' thing ever."

She'd talked Jo into a quiet drink at Shaker's after work, knocked back two cosmopolitans, then pulled a compilation CD of female empowerment anthems out of her handbag and persuaded the DJ to play them.

Mired in her own Mexican standoff with Dan, Jo hadn't the heart to say no to Delwyn's post-Wayne recovery plan, even when her sales rep dragged in fresh recruits—Dan's sister Meredith and Pat, who'd been having a quiet dinner in the adjoining restaurant.

So far, they'd danced to "Sisters Are Doing It For Themselves," "Ladies' Night" and "Girls Just Want to Have Fun." Three of the four were drunk. And it was only 8:15 p.m.

Resolutely, Jo pushed her cocktail aside in favor of her water glass. Delwyn plonked her highball on the table and frowned. "Why aren't you drinking your Sloe Comfortable Screw?"

Across the circular table, Meredith smothered a laugh, drawing the sales rep's attention. "See, Merry, Merry—" leaning forward, she tucked her bright pink cocktail parasol behind Meredith's ear "—I told you it's fun be'n' unattached."

Dan's younger sister was a very pretty woman but with her dark hair pulled back and wearing a conservative yellow blouse, the gaudy parasol made her look like a spinster on her last prayer.

At the reminder that she'd just separated from her husband, Merry sucked on her straw like it was an intravenous drip delivering morphine. The sound spurred Delwyn to another slug of her own drink. "Wonder what Wayne's doing?" she said sadly.

The mechanic had put down his tools and listened politely when Jo had tried to mediate, then equally politely told her to mind her own business. "Like I'm minding mine with you and Dan."

She couldn't argue with his logic. "Just keep the lines of communication open," she'd advised. "That's how we're working things out." Yeah, right. She'd left the garage feeling like a hypocrite. As friends she and Dan had always been able to work through stalemates, but as lovers they were treading new ground—all of it mined.

Jo found herself reaching for her cocktail again and in desperation, picked up a congealing cheesy potato wedge from the shared bowl on the table.

Spending more time with Dan had only

reinforced her conviction that they should wait. He barely slept, worked himself to the bone and made love with an intensity that initially made Jo wonder if, despite his optimism about her cancer, the possibility of a recurrence haunted him. When she'd raised the subject he'd finally admitted he was fighting depression over Steve and Lee's deaths.

His unresolved guilt was another good reason not to get married, but he flat out refused to talk about it again. It was sensible to wait and Dan didn't want to be sensible. He wanted to throw himself into commitment. And while Jo loved him for his courage, she wouldn't be swept into doing something that might be the opposite of what he needed.

Desperate for a cocktail, Jo crunched on a piece of ice.

Delwyn's gold bangles rattled as she plonked her empty highball on the table. "So anyway, Merry, all I'm saying is, why buy the pig, all for a li'l saus—" She broke off, her brown eyes lighting up as "It's Raining Men" started booming over the sound system. "Oh, I *love* this song. I hope the male stripper uses it."

Jo choked on her ice. "You ordered a stripper? For tonight?"

"Why should I miss out jus' because I'm not having a hen night anymore?"

"Does Anton know?" She looked for the bar manager, spotted him polishing glasses.

"Phfft," said Delwyn.

From the dance floor, Dan's mother hollered drunkenly, "Girls, get out here!"

Meredith shrank back in her seat. "Not again."

"Coming!" called Jo and shoved Delwyn out of the booth. "You got her this way, you go dance with her." Obligingly, Delwyn boogied on over, snagging a couple guys en route.

Jo signaled Anton and broke the good news about the stripper. Shaking his head, he reached for his cell. On the dance floor Pat started a conga line, her platinum hair swinging. Her daughter watched in awe.

"I've never seen Mom like this," Meredith confided. "I'm starting to think she might actually care about Dad…I mean as a person, not just out of habit."

Jo knew what she meant. For Pat to loosen up meant a seismic shift was taking place. "I really hope they work it out." It seemed unlikely. Herman had only returned with Merry and her two kids a couple of days ago and was avoiding his estranged wife.

Noticing Meredith twisting her wedding ring, Jo asked gently, "Any chance of reconciliation for you and Charlie?"

Meredith shook her head and sucked so hard on her straw that the ice rattled in the bottom of her glass. "I need another one of these." No one knew the details of her separation, not even her twin in New York.

"Here." Jo slid her untouched cocktail across the table. "Have mine."

Emboldened by alcohol, Merry finally asked the question Jo knew she'd been dying to. "Are you really going to stand my brother up at the altar next week?"

"It won't come to that," she said firmly. "Ross will help me talk sense into him." Jo glanced at her watch. "Dan is picking him up from the bus station now. They should be here any minute."

Ross was Jo's last hope. If he wouldn't help convince Dan to cancel the wedding, she'd leave town the day before the ceremony.

Meredith glanced nervously at the door. "They're coming *here?*"

"We're going to need reinforcements with Pat."

Merry scrambled for her bag. "I'm calling a cab."

"Relax," said Jo. "I know he's Charlie's brother but we're talking the Iceman, remember? Ross will be cool. And only an idiot would hold you responsible for the breakup."

Meredith began twisting her wedding ring.

"The thing is," she began, then stopped as her mother bopped toward them.

"Get ready for some action, girls. The stripper's finally arrived."

Looking to where Pat was pointing, Jo saw Delwyn approaching a muscle-bound hunk standing at the door. "This is going to be interesting."

The new arrival stepped into the light and Pat stifled a tipsy giggle. "Oh, how funny!"

Meredith gulped. "Ross," she said faintly.

Delwyn cupped a hand to her mouth and yelled a question above the music. Ross inclined his head and listened politely. One corner of his mouth twitched, but otherwise nothing about the Iceman's demeanor suggested he was being asked if he got naked for a living.

He might have the body for it but to Jo everything about Ross Coltrane screamed soldier, from his bearing and close-cropped dark hair to the uncompromising line of his jaw. He lifted his gaze and met hers. Even his eyes were battleship gray.

Of all the men in Dan's SAS family, Ross was the one Jo liked least.

"I've never understood the appeal of the strong silent type," she confessed when Dan first asked what she thought of his troop mate. He'd killed himself laughing.

"That's because you're so alike. Both smart, pig-headed, loyal and laws unto yourselves." Jo hadn't appreciated that.

But now, seeing the gaunt cheekbones and heavy limp as Ross started toward her, she swallowed a lump in her throat. He'd hate pity as much as she did, so she forced herself to keep her welcoming hug casual. "Just in time to buy the next round, Coltrane."

"Is that before or after I take my clothes off?"

"I thought you guys were trained to multi-task?"

The music stopped as the DJ took a break. Ross's grin faded as he caught sight of Meredith. Ignoring her, he turned to greet Pat, who was tugging on his arm with tipsy dismay. "Oh, Ross, my poor boy, sit down. You look terr—"

"Mom," Dan cut in harshly as he joined them, and Pat recollected herself. Swaying slightly, she patted her hair, as though aware of her dishevelment.

"Ignore me, Ross," she said with dignity. "I'm a little drunk." She saw her son's disapproval and giggled. "Oh, lighten up," she said. "We've having such fun. We've been dancing and drinking…what was it again, sweetie?"

Delwyn moved closer to Ross. "A Sloe Comfortable Screw," she told him. "Against the

Wall, with a Kiss. That's with Galliano and Amaretto."

Dan half groaned, half laughed. "No wonder you're all tanked." He sat beside Jo and dropped a kiss on her mouth. His lips were cold from being outside. In the overheated fug of the bar, he smelled of fresh air and cypress. He was breaking her heart. "It's encouraging to see you're still sober."

"I'm trying to take a more mature approach to my troubles these days."

"What's that supposed to mean?" Three drunken and unhappy women frowned at her.

"C'mon, Pat." Delwyn tucked her arm through her new best friend's. "Les' go ask the DJ if he'll play 'Girls Jus' Wanna Have Fun' again."

Ross sat down next to his sister-in-law. "Don't you want to join them?" He tweaked the parasol behind her ear.

Blushing, Meredith yanked it out. "Delwyn put it there."

Jo frowned at Ross. "Merry's been a really good sport about this."

"I'll bet."

CHAPTER FIFTEEN

DAN LOOKED BETWEEN his sister and his friend. "Am I missing something?" Normally they got on like a house on fire.

Merry folded her arms. "Have I told you, Danny, how much I appreciate you staying out of my marriage?"

Ross narrowed his eyes. "If that's a dig at me for taking my brother—"

"Taking him in is fine." Merry turned on him. "It's the advice I object to!"

He snorted. "The facts pretty much speak for themselves, so don't play pious—"

Reaching across the table, Dan laid a hand on his friend's forearm. "Why don't you go get the beers?"

Without another word, Ross stood and limped toward the bar.

Dan looked at his sister. "What the hell was that about?"

She deflated like a balloon. "Call me a cab."

"When I've got answers."

Knowing it wouldn't work on him, Merry looked plaintively at Jo.

His lover folded. "I'm on it." She nudged him to let her out of the booth. "Be gentle," she murmured as she passed. Tonight she wore a navy jersey dress that flowed over every curve and as Dan watched her walk away he noticed he wasn't the only male appreciating that. *Sorry, guys, she's taken.*

Jo didn't know yet that Ross was Dan's best man. Like she didn't know that the first of their wedding guests were arriving tonight. Of course, he'd expected to have his reluctant bride on side by now. He should have guessed she'd be stubborn about this.

Dan returned his attention to his little sister, wishing her twin were here to sort her out. But Viv was in New York designing costumes for a Broadway show that opened next week.

"Talk to me," he said more quietly, following Jo's advice. "What *don't* I know about this breakup?"

Tears brimmed in her big brown eyes. "Please, Danny, I can't cope with a postmortem right now."

"Okay," he said reluctantly and handed her a cocktail napkin. "But whatever it is, I'm on your side."

Merry dabbed her eyes. "Even though one of your best mates is on the other?"

That could be a problem, but it wasn't hers. "Ross and I will work it out."

Jo waved from the door.

"Taxi's here, go get your coat. I'll make sure Mom gets home safely."

Tortured singing drew their attention to the dance floor. Arms around each other, Pat and Delwyn were singing at the top of their voices. "…take from me…Herman an' Wayne can't trample on our digg-ni-ty."

"Oh, God."

"I'll send Dad back," Merry promised. Herman was babysitting his grandkids.

"Maybe seeing her like this will shock some sense into him."

"I hope so." Merry gave him a hug before she left. "You've got enough on your plate talking Jo into the wedding. I won't let Ross rile me again."

"I'll talk to him, don't worry."

He waited until his sister joined Jo then strode to the bar where Ross had lined up two beers on the brushed steel surface. What concerned Dan most was that a year ago the Iceman would have kept his feelings to himself.

Ross had been so badly injured that medics hadn't thought he'd live, let alone walk. But like Jo, the guy didn't recognize limitations. His relentless reconditioning regime was driven by the burning ambition to get back on active service.

He'd always been the consummate soldier, totally professional, dispassionate, even clinical in his duties. Ross would never let something as paltry as emotion ride him. Now he seemed to slow-burn with a cold rage that worried his superiors. As yet, they didn't need to make a decision about active duty, but when they did... and if they consulted Dan...

He rubbed his temple, knowing he'd have to argue against his friend's redeployment. One ambush, two deaths and the course of so many people's lives changed.

Dan pulled up a stool. "Mind explaining why you're picking on my sister?"

"Charlie's really hurting over this."

"And Merry's not?" His friend's mouth tightened. "Oh, c'mon, Ross, this is Saint Meredith we're talking about. She's been running after your little brother since the day they met."

"Hey, he's never asked her to."

"Or stopped her, either." Dan picked up his glass.

"At least he didn't kiss someone else."

CHAPTER SIXTEEN

DAN'S BEER WENT DOWN the wrong way and Ross had to thump him on the back. "She hasn't told you, has she?"

"Not yet," he wheezed, "and I don't want to hear it from you."

"Don't trust my version?"

"Don't trust Charlie. I assume that's where you got it."

"You calling my baby brother a liar?"

"You calling my baby sister unfaithful?"

There was a tight silence. Both men gulped some beer. "Only one way to deal with this, Shep." Ross put down his chilled glass and wiped his palms against his jeans. Dan followed suit.

Ross thrust out a hand. "Never speak of this again." They shook on it. Picked up their beers again. "And to think you called me a cynic," Ross added, "when I turned your other sister down for a date."

Sipping his beer, Dan recalled his friend's reasoning at the time. "Yeah, there are sparks with Viv," Ross had admitted, "but I don't want our friendship caught in the crossfire when it turns to shit. It's bad enough that my brother is marrying into your family."

"You were right," Dan said. "I was wrong. I'll never question your judgment again."

"What if I told you to back off this wedding?" Dan scowled. "Thought not," said Ross mildly. "Explain to me again why you're trying to marry an unwilling woman?"

"She's not unwilling…" To hell with it, Dan badly needed an ally. "Jo had cancer…thinks she's doing me a favor by trying to protect me."

Ross's expressionless gaze went to Jo, who was talking to Anton at the other end of the bar. He took another sip of his beer. "What time am I due at the suit rental place tomorrow?"

Dan relaxed. "Ten."

"I can't believe Nate's not here."

The mirror behind the row of liquor bottles showed two guys sharing a drink. It should have been five. Dan raised his glass. "To absent friends."

"To absent friends."

The ale found its way down his constricted throat. It didn't make sense that Nate had cut himself off from his surviving SAS brothers, but then neither did Dan's sense of dread.

He'd believed if he devoted himself to living a meaningful life that he'd conquer his feelings of hopelessness over Steve and Lee's deaths. Single-minded dedication had always worked in the SAS. You committed to a mission, and regardless of setbacks, you never wavered from your objective.

But his marriage mission had only intensified his dread, and Dan couldn't say why.

"I'm starting to think it's more than grief with Nate," he said to Ross.

The other man frowned. "I wish I could remember what happened but I was out cold most of it."

"Nate did everything right. More than right. There's no reason for him to feel it."

"Feel what?"

"Guilt."

Ross whistled silently. "You really think that's what it is?"

Dan nodded.

"I guess you'd recognize the signs."

He forced himself to return his friend's piercing gaze. "I'm over it," he lied.

"Good. Because you don't want that bullshit tainting what you have with Jo. That would be a tragedy and we've had enough of that this past year." Ross raised his glass again. "To everything there is a season," he said softly and Dan recognized the scripture he'd quoted at Steve's funeral. "And this is your time to sow, farmboy." His gaze shifted over Dan's shoulder. "And to dance."

"What?"

Pat seized his arm. "Come boogie with your mother. That spoilsport bar manager canceled our stripper so we'll have to make our own fun."

Dan looked down at her flushed face and that awful hair that made her look like a cougar. His mother was *not* someone he wanted on the prowl. "Why don't you sit down and rest?"

"Pooh!" she said. "I could dance all night. And I'm not accepting excuses… Well, Ross has an excuse but—"

"Fine," Dan cut her off. "Let's get this over with." If she didn't dance with him she might dance with someone who actually fancied her. Where the hell was Herman?

Before he followed Pat he turned back to Ross. "And what season is it for you?"

"A time to heal." But they both knew healing was only a means to an end. Ross was bent on reprisal.

Thank God nothing had happened between Ross and Viv, thought Dan as he walked to the dance floor. His friend was a time bomb waiting to explode and Dan didn't want either of his little sisters anywhere near the detonation zone.

ROSS COLTRANE DIDN'T LIKE being a passenger, at least not when Jo was driving.

He gripped the handhold above the car door whenever she accelerated and shoved his good foot on an imaginary brake every time they reached an intersection.

Hiding a smile, she took a corner sharply enough to drag a squeal from the tires.

Ross's arrogant air of male superiority had always punched her girl-power buttons. It had become a perverse challenge…trying to wring a whimper out of the Iceman.

He slanted her a sidelong glance but didn't say a word. They'd always had this rivalry, ever since he'd first realized Dan's best friend Jo was a girl. He still couldn't fathom that. He was a man's man, with no real interest in women except between the sheets.

She went over a speed bump a little faster than she should and his head hit the ceiling.

From her supine position along the backseat, Delwyn said faintly, "You're making me feel sick."

"Oh, hon, I'm sorry." Contrite, Jo eased her foot off the accelerator. She'd almost forgotten she had a second passenger, she'd been so eager to seize the opportunity to speak to Ross away from Dan when she'd offered to drop him at the farm. Dan was left waiting for Herman. "How about some fresh air?" Pressing a switch on the driver's door, she opened the back window and a chill blast lanced through the car's interior.

Delwyn's disheveled head popped up in the rearview mirror. Propping herself against the passenger door she stuck her face out into the black night with a groan, her long hair flapping back like the ears of a cocker spaniel.

Ross swung around to assess her, then shrugged off his jacket and passed it over. "Put this on to keep warm."

"I'm never drinking cocktails again," she moaned. "I'm sticking to Asti Spumante or beer."

"It's only another couple blocks," Jo reassured them. She really didn't want Delwyn throwing up in her car.

Ross turned back to the front. "It would serve you right for trying to wind me up, Swannie."

"Then quit acting like you're being driven by Miss Daisy." Over her shoulder she called to Delwyn. "If you can't wait to throw up, hon, use Ross's jacket."

His mouth twitched and his incongruous

dimple appeared. "All ammo for the best man's wedding speech, Bridezilla."

Ross had been roped into best man? "Lucky it's not going to happen, then," she retorted. "You and I are having a serious talk." Jo parked in Delwyn's driveway and got out of the car. Ross did the same. "It's okay, I've got her," she said.

Ignoring Jo, Ross opened Delwyn's door. She was leaning against it and toppled sideways with a tipsy giggle. "Oops!"

He caught her falling weight, instinctively bracing on his bad leg. A grimace of pain tightened his features. Diving forward, Jo propped Delwyn to a sitting position.

"Don't you ever listen to good advice?"

"I'm fine." Under the motion-activated outdoor lights his face was ashen.

"Let me guess," she said, exasperated. "Pain is weakness leaving the body." It was a favorite saying of the Special Forces. And in Jo's view, an idiotic one.

"You've got a smart mouth on you, Swannie."

"And you're a stubborn alpha-hole. Go wait in the car."

Shaking his head, Ross bent to hook one of Delwyn's arms over his shoulder. "I'm not leaving you to carry her by yourself. Swing your feet to the ground, that's it, Delwyn... She must have a good stone on you."

Delwyn's lolling head snapped upright; she fixed Ross with a stare of bleary indignation. "Escuse *me,* but I los' two and a quarter pounds on my wedding diet."

"Well, I think you *look* at least five pounds lighter," Jo soothed, slinging Delwyn's other arm around her neck. "Doesn't she, Ross?"

"I didn't see her before," he said with annoying male truthfulness. "On the count of three. One...two...three!"

They hauled Delwyn upright and she hung between them like a sack of potatoes.

"C'mon, sweetie," Jo encouraged. She'd forgotten that drunks were deadweights. "We need you to walk now."

"Jus' wanna go to sleep."

"Only a few steps, I promise...you don't want to wake your flatmate, do you?"

"Don' care," said Delwyn. "Don' care 'bout anything now Wayne's dumped me."

Inside she shrugged off Jo's arm and collapsed on Ross' chest. "You wanna have sex? That'll show Wayne." She hitched up a shoulder strap and licked her lips to make them shiny. "I mean, you do think I'm hot, right?"

Jo prayed Ross heard the plaintiveness in her voice.

"I think you're gorgeous," he said.

Delwyn beamed and flapped an arm in Jo's direction. "Go 'way."

I don't think so.

"But the thing is, Delwyn," Ross lifted her off his chest, "you've seen me limping, right?"

She rolled her head to look at his leg. "Uh-huh."

"Well…the…accident also affected my ability to satisfy a woman. Otherwise I'd be all over you."

Jo hid a smile.

"Really?" Delwyn clutched his shirt.

"Really."

"Can I tell Wayne that? I mean you being hot for me, not about—you know."

"That depends. How big is Wayne?" Delwyn indicated a picture in a heart-shaped frame on the mantel. Even the wrench in his hand couldn't make the lanky mechanic look menacing. "Sure," Ross said generously. "You can tell him."

Delwyn's flatmate came out from the bathroom, clutching a towel around her, then fluffed up her wet hair as she caught sight of Ross. "What's going on?" Delwyn burst into tears.

"I want Wayne," she wailed.

Leaving her to her flatmate's ministrations, they made their escape. "You can be nice,"

Jo said as they walked back to the car. "Who knew?"

"Yeah, like I told Dan…you and I are nothing alike."

She laughed. "And the impotence thing was inspired."

"I'm glad you found that amusing." The flatness of his tone gave rise to a terrible suspicion. No, thought Jo, Dan would have told me.

Assuming Ross had confided in him.

Unsure what to think, she changed the subject. "Dan said you want to go back…to operations, I mean."

Ross clipped his seat belt. "As soon as the scars heal." Unconsciously, he massaged one fist and her skin prickled. The Iceman was the last person she'd expect to see in the thrall of revenge.

Disturbed, Jo refastened her own seat belt and started the engine. She knew from her mastectomy that external healing was the easiest part of the recovery journey. It was the internal scars, the ones you refused to acknowledge, that held you back. And she sensed Ross hadn't even begun that process.

This week it had become increasingly apparent that neither had Dan.

When he'd first joined the SAS, Jo had been a little jealous of Dan's bond with his fellow soldiers until it hit her that these guys held his life in their hands every time they were deployed. The closer the bond, the better their odds.

Which was why the survivors were suffering so much now. Not only had they lost buddies closer than brothers, they'd failed to keep one another safe.

However ambivalent she might feel about Ross personally, Jo would never question his loyalty to Dan. In fact she was banking on it.

"I'm worried about him, Ross," she said abruptly. "I think Dan holds himself culpable. But he wasn't with you on patrol and he couldn't have done anything if he was." Taking her eyes off the road, she glanced his way. "Could he?"

He was silent a moment. They'd left suburbia and were on country roads. No streetlights to illuminate his profile. "Do you know why we called him Shep?"

"I assume because he's a farmboy."

Ross shook his head. "It's short for the good shepherd. As our signaler, it was always Dan's job to get us in." He eased his leg forward. "And get us out. He knows there's no reason to blame himself, he knows he would probably have been another casualty. I've told him that. But he doesn't feel it. And feelings don't disappear just because you apply logic."

"Love isn't a cure-all," said Jo, "but I think Dan expected it to be. His faith in my ability to heal him is touching but—"

"It's misplaced," Ross supplied. "The only person who can forgive him for not being with us is himself."

"You've got to help me talk him out of this wedding," she said desperately. "He's not making rational decisions right now."

"Are you?"

"You tell me since apparently we're so much alike," she snapped.

Ross smiled. "I'll help you," he said, and Jo unclenched her hands on the steering wheel.

"Thank you."

"And in return…"

Jo took her foot off the accelerator.

CHAPTER SEVENTEEN

"MIJN GOD!" ACROSS the bar, Herman gaped at his wife, currently hiking her orange skirt up to her knees so she could climb onto a barstool.

Dan shrugged. "I did tell you about the hair last week," he reminded his father.

Herman's eyes widened as Pat called loudly for another drink. "Yes, but…but blond not… not…"

"Tarty?" Dan suggested. "Vampish, slutty?"

"Common," growled his father. "And your *moeder* is not common. Why are you still letting her drink?"

"Anton's been secretly feeding her nonalcoholic cocktails for the past hour. Mom only thinks she's getting drunker. What took you so long?" Dan was irritable. He'd sent Ross off with Jo half an hour ago because Ross needed to get that injured leg elevated, not that he'd appreciated the reminder. Steve's widow, Claire, and her son, Lewis, were arriving sometime after 9:30 p.m. He needed to be there to welcome them. Hell, he needed to tell Jo they were here for the wedding. Hopefully she'd have dropped Ross off and left before they arrived.

After his houseguests were settled he'd drive back to her place. Dan didn't sleep well, but he slept even worse without Jo in his arms. He'd break the news to her in the morning before he returned to the farm to make breakfast.

Any way you looked at it, things were getting complicated.

"I took so long," grumbled Herman, "because I got a flat tire. I don't know why I'm here anyway. It's not like your mother even wants me."

Catching sight of him, Pat scowled. Tossing her head, she swung around to the counter and started talking animatedly to the next person in the queue for drinks, a middle-aged man who looked at her bemusedly.

"You see," said Herman gruffly and turned to go.

"Oh, for God's sake," Dan said. "Wait here."

He strode over to his mother. "Okay, Blondie. Are you going to keep channeling Monroe or put some of those psychology books to use and save your marriage."

The ditzy airhead changed back into his mother. "I'm scared, Danny. I don't know if there's anything left to save."

"Feel the fear and do it anyway, Mom." He

helped her off the stool but when they turned around, his father had already gone. Shit. "We'll catch him in the parking lot." Hand under Pat's elbow, he hustled her outside. Herman was twenty paces ahead.

"Dad! Wait up."

Herman kept walking. Dan urged his resistant mother faster. A couple of yards away from her husband, she pulled free. "That's right, Herman Jansen, make me run after you. Again!"

Herman stopped. "Looked to me like you were running after some other guy two minutes ago."

"Oh, c'mon," said Dan. "He was twenty years younger."

His mother narrowed her eyes. "Are you saying I had no chance?"

"God, I hope not."

"Well, I hope you get lucky this time," Herman spluttered. "Heaven forbid you have to suffer another thirty-five years trying to make a silk purse of a sow's ear. Maybe this guy will share his feelings and go to art galleries and finally make you happy."

Pat's eyes glittered with tears. "Maybe he'll care enough about me to fight for me, too."

"Hey, I wasn't the one who asked for a divorce," Herman accused her. "I'm not the one gallivanting around town telling anyone who'd listen how goddamn fine I am about our separation. I'm not the one getting drunk and flirting in bars." Bewildered, he asked, "What am I supposed to read from that?"

"That she loves and misses you and wants you back," Dan interjected. "Isn't it freaking obvious that she's only been kicking up to get your attention?" Honestly, how had his father learned so little about women when he'd raised two daughters?

Pat didn't answer.

Dan coaxed her closer to Herman. "And you seem to forget that she stuck by you for thirty-five years as a farmer's wife. And maybe she begrudged that sacrifice sometimes...okay a lot—"

"You can stop now, Danny," Pat interrupted.

Doggedly he continued. "But she made the best of it most of the time, didn't she?"

His father looked at his mother. It was a strange look, almost of compassion.

Pat bowed her head. "No," she admitted. "I didn't."

There was a short, tight silence.

"If you come back now, *lieveling,*" Herman said softly, "you'll never know who you were meant to be. I'll end up the scapegoat again and I don't deserve that."

Pat looked up. "No, you don't," she agreed.

"Wait a minute," said Dan, "am I hearing you both right? You're giving up on thirty-five years of marriage just like that?"

"Sometimes admitting defeat takes more courage than going on," said his father. "But you're too young to understand that. Patricia, I can still give you a ride home."

She straightened her shoulders and forced a smile. "Thank you, Herman."

His father helped his mother into the car with the same gallantry he'd always shown her. When he closed the door, Dan stopped him.

"But, Dad," he said, confused. "You don't want this."

"No, son." Herman smiled sadly. "Unfortunately that doesn't mean it isn't the right thing to do."

JO WAS IN THE FARMHOUSE kitchen making two hot chocolates while Ross took a shower. She heard the rumble of a familiar engine on the driveway—it had been a long time but she still knew the sound of that Caddy.

She reached the porch just as Claire got out of her late husband's fifties Coupe de Ville. Jo had talked to Steve's widow half a dozen times over the past year, but this was the first time since his death they'd caught up in person. Claire's smile wobbled as she approached; so did Jo's. Then they were wrapping their arms around each other and holding tight. They rocked like that for a moment then Claire murmured "Lewis" and they broke apart.

Swallowing tears, Jo peered into the back window for Claire's thirteen-year-old son. Moonlight revealed his face half buried in a pillow as he slept. "Out cold," she reported. "Dan can carry him in when he gets back." Tucking her arm through Claire's she led her inside and settled her at the kitchen table with Ross's hot chocolate. "Am I allowed to ask how you're doing?" she said gently.

Claire Langford had always been an ethereal beauty, fine boned with long blond hair and delicate features. Only her eyes gave a clue to her character, being a fearless Viking blue. Now they were wary and sad. "To tell the truth, I cope best by concentrating on other people's lives.… How's your grandmother?"

Jo took the hint. "Slowly settling in at Pinehill." She found another mug for Ross, filled it with milk and spooned in some chocolate powder. "She's becoming less aware of her condition, so happier I think. But again, I could be projecting," she added ruefully. "It's difficult to tell."

"Is she coming to the wedding?"

Jo sighed. "Please tell me that's not why you're here."

"It's off?"

"It's never been on."

Sitting down, she told Claire the truth. All of it. She reacted as Dan had. "You should have let us know when you were first diagnosed."

"I guess I still have something to learn about relying on other people," she said.

Claire was silent and Jo let it lie. She knew Dan was frustrated by Claire's refusal to accept support. The SAS had a trust that provided financial assistance to widows, but emotionally she was going it alone.

"Anyway you can see why I want to wait." Choosing a pink marshmallow to annoy Ross, Jo put the mug in the microwave and keyed in a minute and a half. "At least until my odds of survival are closer to normal people's."

"I can see you want to protect him," Claire said slowly. "But Dan's going into this with his eyes open. Just like I did when I married an SAS trooper. And hard as it is now, I still wouldn't trade those fourteen years with Steve for fifty with anyone else." She put down her mug and smiled. "I know I've just made things harder for you, but think about it."

Before Jo could respond, the back door

opened and Dan walked in. "Claire, I'm so sorry I wasn't here when you arrived." Warily he looked at Jo but she was still too shaken by what Claire had said to challenge him on their so-called wedding guests.

"Not a problem." Claire returned his awkward hug. "It gave Jo and me a chance to catch up. Before I left Mom finally told me your parents split up. Why am I the last to know?"

Dan's smile grew fixed. "We didn't want to worry you." This self-consciousness wasn't like him.

"Like I told her, I'm a widow, not an invalid," said Claire, an edge to her voice.

"Of course not," Dan said heartily.

Jo rescued him. "Lewis is asleep in the car. Can you carry him in?"

He left with obvious relief. Jo looked at Claire, who shrugged. "He's acted like this ever since Steve died."

Ross limped into the kitchen, drying his hair on a towel. "Hey, Claire, didn't hear you arrive."

His greeting was more natural, but if anything Ross's solicitude surpassed Dan's. No wonder Claire avoided these guys, Jo thought. They were as suffocating as helicopter parents.

After Dan settled Lewis they sat talking at

the table, where Jo kept up a semblance of normalcy by picking on Ross. Claire was patently grateful, Ross gave as good as he got, but Dan became twitchy.

"Jo, I'll walk you to your car," he said after fifteen minutes.

"You understood what I was doing, right?" she said when they were outside. "Normalizing things until you relax around Claire…and Ross." She smiled. "I swear when you gave him that cushion for his leg he was seriously contemplating ramming it down your throat."

"I know your heart's in the right place," he said carefully.

"Dan, what's going on?" She diverted him into the barn and switched on the light. Work benches, farm equipment and the ATV came into sharp focus. "You can't stop treating Ross like an invalid. Every time I touched you in front of Claire you pulled away."

"I'm just trying to be sensitive," he said. "She and Steve were always hugging and holding hands."

Jo tried to read his expression but even under stark fluorescent overheads it was shuttered. "By making such a big deal about showing me affection, you're only drawing more attention to her loss."

"We don't have to rub her nose in the fact that we're happy, do we?"

Happy? Jo nearly laughed. Happy in desperate snatches maybe, both conscious of the looming wedding, both deferring a final showdown. But they couldn't go on like this. "Dan—"

He cut her off, obviously aware he'd made a tactical error. "Like I said, your heart's in the right place, but some of the things you said to Ross tonight were kind of on the nose."

At this, Jo did laugh. "Ross lives for conflict. And we always take potshots at each other. You think he'd want me to go easy on him because he's in rehab? He hates being treated as a invalid."

"Is that a dig at me?"

"No." Still smiling, she put her arms around his waist. "Well, maybe a small one."

His arms stayed by his sides. "So you know Ross better than I do now, is that it?"

"Hey." She gave him a gentle shake. "Deep breaths. You're overreacting."

He huffed out a long sigh of frustration, but returned her embrace. "Let's back off this because I don't want to fight with you unless we can have make-up sex afterward."

"Drive over when everyone's in bed." Since Herman's return their sleepovers had moved to her place anyway. They needed to talk…

really talk, not make love and pretend they were changing each other's minds. Claire was here for the wedding. Jo had to challenge him on that and a cold drafty barn wasn't the place to do it.

"I can't." He told her what had happened with his parents. "I should stay here, wait for Dad."

And though she suspected he was buying time, Jo kissed him, because tonight he needed support not confrontation. Besides, Ross had said he'd help her; she had to give him that opportunity.

DAN MOVED THROUGH THE next thirty hours feeling like a bad actor in a parody of his life.

He frowned when he should have laughed and he laughed when he should have been serious. He was uncomfortable in his own skin.

And despite his best efforts, he was unable to connect with the people he most cared about, particularly the woman he was trying to talk into marrying him.

But the worst torture was spending time with his godson. Unlike the adults, the boy couldn't pretend things would get better. His sorrow stripped Dan of every rationalization and left him nowhere to hide.

The laughing enthusiast that Dan remembered

had been replaced by an apathetic, taciturn teen who responded to his clumsy attempts to jolly him along with surly distrust. Claire desperately tried to laugh it off. Lewis looked at him like he didn't know him anymore and Dan, trapped in this agonizing caricature of himself, didn't blame him.

But doggedly, he kept trying.

This morning—Sunday—they were going duck-shooting, just the two of them, like Dan had promised. He'd been up since five getting gear ready even though they didn't need to be in position by the farm's pond until sunrise at seven-twenty.

At six forty-five the kid still wasn't up even though Dan had personally set his alarm for six-thirty. On stocking feet, he crept past Ross's bedroom door. He was staying behind. It wouldn't be fair on the ducks, he'd said with his usual modesty, but Dan suspected his buddy felt too tempted to shoot him.

"Back off," he'd advised last night. "Back off nagging me to rest, back off smothering Claire, back off playing Mr. Hearty with Lewis. If I were you I'd concentrate on wooing my reluctant bride. I've bought you time to close the deal by saying I'd help her. Don't blow it. I'm starting to think you don't deserve Jo, and given how much she and I like making each other suffer, that's saying something."

But for the first time Dan was suffering doubts about his ability to win her over.

Which is why he'd fobbed her off last night. "Duck-shooting at dawn, things to organize. I'll come over afterward, we'll talk."

Jo had carried him since Claire and Lewis's arrival, smoothing over the conversational rough spots, filling any awkward silences and patiently accepting his physical withdrawal because as hard as Dan tried, he couldn't be natural in front of Claire. She'd carried him and he despised himself for letting her.

Quietly, so as not to wake Claire in the adjoining bedroom, he tapped on Lewis's door and opened it to darkness. He must have turned off the alarm and gone back to sleep. Closing the door behind him, Dan switched on the light.

"Ow, what did you do that for?" The boy buried his blond head under the pillow. Dan had borrowed extra beds from his mother.

"Hey, mate, we're going duck-shooting, remember?"

Blinking, Lewis sat up. His eyes might be adjusting to the light but it was obvious he'd been wide-awake. "I've changed my mind. Go without me."

"But you were keen last night." An exaggeration—resigned was more accurate.

"I'm tired and it's a long way to walk." This from the kid who used to run everywhere.

"C'mon," Dan coaxed. "The fresh air will do you good. You've hardly been out of the house since you arrived." Instead he'd spent most of his time on the internet playing RuneScape.

The teen's mouth turned sulky. "So you're going to make me, is that it?"

"Of course not." Dan tamped down his disappointment. "But…last year you were looking forward to this."

"That was last year. Anyway I'll be useless."

"You don't know that. Besides, I'll teach you."

"Nah, I'll stay here."

Dan steeled himself. "Does it make you feel sad…because your Dad was going to do this with you?" *It makes me sad*.

Scowling, Lewis flung himself on his side, hauling up the blankets. "You sound just like Mom, making a drama out of it. Not everything relates back to Dad dying. And why do I have to be his clone…with all the same interests and stuff?"

Dan was shocked. "No one expects you to be."

Lewis curled into a tight ball. "I'm tired of people doing things with me because they feel sorry for me, all right?"

"Louie," Dan said helplessly.

"You didn't even want to invite us," Lewis accused, his green eyes hostile. "I heard Mom tell Grandma. Our invitation came ages after everyone else's. You only asked us because you thought you should. Dad's the one you cared about."

He'd heard enough. "I'm sorry, but that's bullshit!"

Lewis blinked but his mulish expression returned. "I don't care anyway." He pulled the blankets over his head.

"Dan?" Claire came in, tying her dressing gown. "What's going on?" She sat on the bed and laid a hand on Lewis's back.

"He's trying to make me go duck-shooting and I don't want to," said Lewis, his voice thick with tears, through the covers. Claire looked at Dan.

Shaking his head, he raised his hands in a gesture of surrender.

"It's okay." She managed a smile. "I'll deal with it…you go."

Go away.

Dan left the house and walked to the pond by

flashlight only realizing when he got there that he'd left all the gear behind. Blue had followed him; he sent the dog home. Switching off the torch, he sat in Herman's maimai—a hide made of wooden framing and corrugated iron covered in brush.

Suffering alone in the dark.

The rain began at dawn, a fine mist that softened the slowly revealed landscape, the pond, marsh and reeds. Through the hide's narrow aperture, Dan watched ripples stir on the water, as fish broke the surface, listened to the first tentative birdsong.

A duck flew in; planing across the pond's surface with its webbed feet angled and wings outstretched, quacking loudly.

The rain gathered force until heavy raindrops bounced off the water's surface and blew under the tin roof. Within ten minutes it was running in a rivulet down one corner post, sending a black spider scurrying from its web.

A drop landed on Dan's head, then another, forcing him to change position. Blood returned to his cramped legs.

I should have been there. He'd nearly said it to Claire, but Steve's widow didn't need the added burden of his regret. Dan buried his face in his hands.

His mother had told him he was broken but he hadn't wanted to believe her.

He did now.

CHAPTER EIGHTEEN

JO WAS MARSHALING her final arguments against the wedding when the doorbell rang. He was early. Taking a deep breath she opened the front door. "You're right," Dan said before she could exhale. "We should postpone the wedding."

It was the last thing Jo had expected to hear and her relief was so overwhelming, she started to laugh. "Thank you. Dan, thank you!" Dragging him inside she peppered his face with kisses. "I was so worried…I mean, I'd even packed a bag to do a runner…" She stopped because his face was drawn and tired. Defeated. Something was terribly wrong.

"What happened?"

He raked a hand through his hair. "I've screwed everything up."

Leading him to the kitchen, she pointed to a chair. "Sit down, I'll make a cup of tea."

Instead he went to the window and looked down out on the garden, while he explained what had happened with Lewis in a flat voice.

"So you'll talk to him," she said quietly,

putting the kettle on. "Make him understand how important he is to you. For his own sake, not just because he's Steve's son."

He was still looking out the window and she followed his gaze. Not a breath of wind stirred the trees; it was like looking at a photograph. "Dan?"

"Live big," he said. When he turned, she could see his self-contempt. "Tell me, Jo, what kind of *loser* says that? Claire and Lewis are suffering, Ross is goddamn handicapped and Nate…who knows where Nate's head's at. And what do I do? Make some hollow vow to honor my dead buddies' memories by chasing happiness. It's pathetic."

"There's nothing wrong with lighting a beacon in the dark."

"If I'd been there, I would have been driving. Instead Steve died—the guy with a wife and kid. It should have been *me,* Jo. I had no dependants."

"Yes you did." Going to him, she gripped his shoulders. "You had me, even if I was just your best friend then. And I don't care if it's selfish, I thank God every day that you survived, Dan. And so does your mother and your father and your sisters."

Removing her hands, he kissed them and brought them to his chest. "I love you," he said.

"So much. But you were right. Part of the reason I've been so desperate to get you to the altar is that I want to move forward…get past pain." Her knuckles ached under the pressure of his grip. "We'll postpone the wedding until I get my shit together. You deserve better than to be dragged through my grieving process."

Only Dan would see his vulnerability as weakness. No, not only Dan. She did that, too. That's what happened when you were stronger than most people. You began to think everything was your responsibility—and your fault.

"To paraphrase my father—" Dan mustered a smile "—sometimes backing off is the right thing to do."

She stared at him. Dan was a protector. He didn't think of adversity as something to be avoided. Claire had tried to tell her that but Jo hadn't wanted to hear it because she was afraid of relying on anyone but herself. The truth was she loved a man who could handle anything her cancer threw at them, who would be strong even when she couldn't. All she had to do was let him. Fear released its hold on her.

"We're not postponing the wedding," she said.

It was his turn to stare. "What?"

"We're not postponing the wedding." Dan wanted to be his best for her; it was in his DNA.

Jo understood that because it was in hers. But she'd learned something when he'd laid his hand against her scar. *I don't care about perfect. I just care that you're here.*

Pulling her hands free, Jo wrapped her arms around his neck. "I love you," she said. "And I need you, Dan." Her laugh was shaky. "God, how long has it taken me to admit that? And I don't care how you come—whole or broken. Like you don't care how I come. Because that's how much we love each other."

"I don't want to come to you broken," he said harshly. "I don't want to marry you doubting my ability to make you happy. I need to believe I can slay any dragons that come up."

"I have no doubt you can slay dragons. None." Releasing him, Jo picked up her bag and went to the door. "I'm due at Pinehill to visit Nan so let's cut to the chase." Her mouth lifted in a tiny smile. "I'll be at the church on Tuesday. All you need to do is decide whether to show up."

She was halfway out the door before his shock wore off. "Of course I'm going to show up if you still want to go through with it." He sounded truly appalled. "What the hell kind of guy do you think I am?"

Jo thought about that the rest of the morning. He was a good strong man who found equilibrium in action and instead fate had forced him into a passive role. Destroyed his faith in his ability to protect the people he loved.

Somehow she had to help him get that faith back. Somehow she had to convince him of hers. Because if at some level he felt he didn't deserve to be happy, there was always the risk he might sabotage their relationship.

And that simply wasn't an option.

MIDAFTERNOON JO DROVE OUT to the farm. She tracked Ross to the barn where Dan had set up some weights. "Should you be bench-pressing alone?"

Biceps straining, he finished his reps, dropped the weight bar back on the stand and sat up, breathing heavily. His tank top was drenched with sweat. "I stay under ninety kilos if I'm by myself."

She handed him the towel draped on a wooden countertop and he wiped his neck.

"You missed our boy," he commented. "He's driven Claire and Lewis into town."

Our boy. It was the first time Ross had acknowledged her as family, the first time he'd included himself on her side. All things became possible. "I know," she admitted. "I set it up with Claire."

While Ross dried his face, she assessed the rope of muscle across his shoulders. "So tell me, Ice-cream, do you think you're recovered enough to take down a man weighing…oh, I don't know…let's say 179 pounds?"

His eyes appeared over the towel. "He said you'd agreed to the wedding?"

"I have." Jo perched on the other end of the bench press. "But we have to get him over this crazy idea that somehow he let you all down."

"So you want me to pound some sense into him? Believe me, if I was fit, I'd try." He grimaced as he massaged his leg through his sweat pants. "Give me another two months."

"I haven't got that kind of time. We're getting married day after tomorrow and I don't want this hanging over us." She hesitated. "I have a plan."

"I'm listening."

"I think Dan needs to prove himself," she began carefully. "I think he needs to be reminded that he's capable of great things when the people he cares about need him. And you said you'd help me."

He stood. "The plan, Jo."

Taking a deep breath, she told him. As she talked, he hauled off his damp tank top and toweled down. Even greyhound-lean through months in hospital, his frame was still powerful, muscle over bone.

When she finished he said nothing. He could

be thinking it over… More likely Ross was contemplating calling for a straitjacket and having her taken away. His expression gave nothing away.

"There's a high risk of failure."

"There has to be. Dan won't buy it unless the stakes are high…and real."

Draping the towel around his shoulders Ross picked up the discarded tank top and gestured toward the farmhouse.

"And if he doesn't make it in time, Jo?" Together, they headed across the yard. "It would make things worse, and not just for Dan. You'd probably lose him."

She was well aware of that. "I believe in him," she said. "And I'm prepared to stake everything on that faith."

He was silent until they reached the stoop. "I can't do it, Jo."

She struggled to hide her disappointment. "Well, it was a crazy idea."

Ross grabbed the handrail, favoring his bad leg as he maneuvered the stairs. "Even with the element of surprise, I'm not fit enough to overpower Dan."

"No. I guess not."

Reaching the top, Ross looked down at her. "That's why we'll need drugs."

A SHOPPING MALL WAS a place Dan normally avoided, but Jo was right. He had to make his peace with Lewis, so when Claire suggested a quick coffee before he headed back to the farm he forced himself to say yes.

She chose a table right in the middle of the food court, which intensified his uneasiness. No soldier liked to sit exposed on all sides. And what was it with these places and their acoustics? Chatter bounced off the walls and floors, amplified and echoed around the domed atrium.

Little kids raced between the inside playground and formica tables, strollers blocked throughways and retirees paused for leisurely conversations outside doorways.

What the hell were these people thinking?

While Claire and Lewis found a seat, he queued to order coffees and a chocolate thickshake and thought about Jo. She'd blindsided him this morning by doing a U-turn on the wedding, and right now Dan didn't know how he felt about it.

No, that wasn't true.

He was gut-plungingly, head-swimmingly relieved she still loved him—and simultaneously terrified of letting her down. His problem wasn't resolved, he hadn't mastered the churning emotions that kept exhausting his reserves. And that scared Dan, it scared him to death. But for Jo's sake he'd fake it.

Out of the corner of his eye he watched Claire talking intently to a sullen Lewis. Even unable to hear, he knew what she was saying. Make an effort…be nice.… *Pretend we're okay.*

Is that how life was for them all now? Pretending?

Lewis's face got darker and darker, it didn't surprise Dan when he flung himself out of his seat and walked off to the men's room, where his mother couldn't follow.

"Teenagers," she said when Dan put down the tray. "I think you'll be glad to see the back of us."

They were staying with Pat tonight so this was his last chance to get this right.

"Not as glad as you'll be to see the back of me, I'm thinking."

Her eyes widened. "Of course not, I—"

"Claire, let's start being honest with each other." Maybe he'd screw this up but Dan was sick of ignoring the elephant in the room. "Let me get Lewis. He needs to hear this, too."

The teen was outside the men's room leaning against the wall, marking time. "I've had enough of this," Dan said. "Come with me."

Back at the table, Lewis changed chairs to

sit next to Claire. It was a poignant gesture, revealing his apprehension.

Dan sat opposite. "Lewis, you were right this morning," he said. "I do feel sorry for you. And having you visit with your mom hurts like hell." Claire's arm crept around her son's rigid shoulders. "The thing is—" Dan kept his attention fixed on the boy's face "—I want to make your pain go away and I can't and that makes me feel helpless. And we guys don't like feeling helpless, do we?"

Lewis jerked his head no.

"Nate and Ross and me, we're missing your dad and Uncle Lee, too, and that means we're not doing such a great job of being what you need right now. But we love you and your mom, you're our family and always will be. I want to help you through this, mate, but you'll have to tell me how… Will you do that for me?"

"I guess," he mumbled.

Dan looked at Claire. "When I know, you'll know," she said hoarsely. "But…keep calling in the meantime."

He smiled at her. "You got it."

"You know, I might go get a muffin," she said shakily. "I'm hungry. Anyone else want one?"

"Sounds good," said Dan. "Lewis?"

"Nah, I'm not hungry."

"But thanks, Mom," Claire prompted.

Lewis rolled his eyes. "Thanks, Mom."

When she had left, the boy looked at Dan. "Do you think that maybe I could come stay sometimes during school holidays, with you and Jo? Help on the farm like you and Dad did for Uncle Herman?" He hesitated. "Sometimes Mom and I need time apart."

"We'd love to have you as long as Claire agrees. But, Lewis, you also need to try harder with your mom. Being sad isn't an excuse for being difficult."

"I know," Lewis said, "but she can't seem to help it."

Fortunately he was busy unwrapping the straw for his thickshake and didn't see Dan raise his eyebrows. Typical bloody teenager, Dan thought, never my fault. "So make allowances for her," he suggested drily. At least he could start smoothing out some of the rough edges when the boy came to stay. His spirits lifted a fraction. Finally, something practical he could do for Claire.

"Yeah, I guess." Lewis punched the straw through the plastic lid. "Um, Dan, will you tell me the truth about something?"

"Yes." It would always be the truth now, however painful.

"Mom told me Dad died right away."

Lewis's throat convulsed as he looked up. "Did she make that up to make me feel better?"

Dan managed not to flinch. "Nate was with Steve and he said your dad died instantly." An inconsistency started niggling at the back of his mind.

"You feel bad because you weren't there, don't you?" The question jerked his attention back to Lewis. The teen shrugged. "I heard Ross and Mom talking."

The truth, he reminded himself. However painful. "Yeah, Lewis, I do."

Lewis picked up his drink and took a sip, set it down. Eyes downcast he said, "It's hard being the one left behind, isn't it?"

For a few seconds, Dan couldn't move, then he reached across the table and squeezed the boy's shoulder. "That's why we all have to look after one another."

"Yeah." In silence they watched the toddlers riot, teenage girls preen, harassed mothers gulp their caffeine fixes and well-dressed retirees pour tea. "Dan?"

"Yeah, mate." He didn't know how much more of this heartrending honesty he could take.

"I'm real glad you didn't die, too."

CHAPTER NINETEEN

DAN STOOD IN THE CHURCH, the air of the vestry scented with honeycomb polish, old wood and an acrid note of incense. Father O'Malley had apologized for the chill but it was a short rehearsal and not worth heating the building, he'd explained.

The cold meant Dan shouldn't be having any trouble staying awake.

He yawned.

"Hell, I'm…I mean, sorry, Father." It hadn't been a very late night. His female relatives had commandeered Jo for some prewedding pampering and a champagne sleepover.

It seemed ironic that when he and his bride were most desperate to spend time together, their wedding got in the way. Ross had forced him on a token stag night with a few mates where Baz had made another futile effort to talk him into the taupe waistcoat and cravat.

Dan didn't think he'd drunk that much alcohol but he'd been feeling off color all morning and the hangover remedy Ross had made him hadn't helped. He covered another yawn.

"Nerves take some people that way," the priest said cheerfully. "My advice is to get a good night's sleep, son. You want to be bright eyed and bushy tailed tomorrow."

Tomorrow. Dan tightened his grip on his bride's hand, then was glad of the support as he experienced a momentary dizziness. Maybe it *was* nerves.

"You okay?" Jo murmured.

"Fine." He'd worried her enough.

The wedding party was a small one. Ross as best man. Delwyn as bridesmaid. A last-minute flower girl because his niece Tilly had begged her way into the job. Jo had decided they should walk down the aisle together.

Feeling himself sway, Dan widened his stance and tried to concentrate as Father O'Malley rambled on, catching only snippets. Flowers handed over…vows…exchange of rings.

"Ross," said the priest, "make sure you carry the bride's ring on your little finger, but, Delwyn, put the groom's ring on your thumb. I can't tell you how many are lost because the maid of honor uses her ring finger."

Yesterday, Jo had turned down an engagement ring, insisting she was happy with the simple white-gold wedding bands he'd already chosen.

On the quiet, Dan had taken hers back to have it set with three diamonds. He'd pick it up after this rehearsal.

He realized he'd zoned out again and tried to concentrate.

"Then you kiss the bride," said Father O'Malley.

"That's definitely worth practicing." Dan leaned toward Jo and found himself gripping her shoulders for support. "Okay, this is embarrassing," he said, "but I'm feeling faint and I need fresh air."

The priest laughed. "That's why we rehearse, son. To take the edge off the nerves. Well, there's only the recessional now, so lead him out, Jo, and see you both tomorrow."

Dan looked at his bride and it seemed as if he was viewing her through a pane of glass. She was watching him anxiously so he tried to smile but his mouth felt as pliable as day-old chewing gum.

"Let's get you outside," she said. "Ross!"

Dan found himself being marched down the aisle between his bride and best man.

"I don't think you're supposed to join us," he joked but he was glad of his friend's hand under his elbow.

"It wasn't supposed to happen this quickly," Jo murmured.

"Shep, you bloody lightweight," Ross muttered.

Dan realized he was leaning on Ross and straightened. "Your leg."

"It's fine… Jo?" Ross's voice was casual. "Go get the car."

They reached the top of the steps and Dan gripped the handrail. "Something's wrong. I can hardly stand up.…"

Jo's VW Polo braked in front of them. She jumped out, leaving the engine running, and opened the back door. "Have a little lie-down, honey."

Dan opened his mouth to argue…couldn't. His lids wouldn't stay open. He took a step forward and stumbled. Jo cried a warning and Ross's arms closed like iron bands around his chest. Briefly he returned to consciousness, felt upholstery leather, cool under his cheek. Backseat…he thought. Now where's Jo?

Then nothing.

As Jo anxiously watched Ross bundle Dan into the back she heard the sound of voices growing louder from inside the church.

"Deal with it," Ross grunted. "I'll meet you around the corner."

Spinning around, she ran up the stairs, pulling

the church doors closed behind her and startling Father O'Malley who was coming up the aisle with Delwyn and Merry, who was supervising the flower girl. "Why can't I wear high heels?" the little girl complained.

"Father," Jo said breathlessly, "I just wanted to ask…" Her mind went blank.

"Yes," he encouraged.

"If—if you'd noticed how much weight Delwyn's lost."

SOUND FILTERED INTO Dan's consciousness. Birdsong. Smells. Dense. Earthy. Woody…a rustle above. Instinctively he rolled, found his nose buried in leaves and shoved himself unsteadily to a crouch, blinking to focus. Identify the enemy.

A native wood pigeon stilled in the miro tree where it had been feasting on berries, its white breast like a flag of surrender, the rest of its metallic-green plumage indistinguishable against the canopy. Dan blinked. Head cocked, the bird blinked back, then with a heavy whir of wings flew off the branch and disappeared.

Still dazed, he sank down on his rump, leaning against a tree while he got his bearings.

Kereru was a forest bird…he was in a forest? His blank gaze took in the surrounding trees…

podocarps mostly, tawa, taraire, puriri and miro. Ancient trees rooted in the land. Light struggled to pierce the chill mist that cloaked the canopies in white. But he wasn't cold.

Dan looked down. He was wearing hiking boots, a Swanndri bush jacket, jeans. He touched his aching head, felt a woolen beanie.

Closing his eyes, he searched his memory. Jo's lips brushing against his. "I believe in you."

The subdued murmurs of strangers, men. "I hope you know what you're doing."

And Ross. "So do I, but she's convinced…" Words lost in the louder thwack, thwack, thwack of helicopter rotor blades. Dan rubbed his forehead. No, he was confused, mixing past with present. He remembered the church, a dry throat and feeling woozy. His eyes snapped open. Dammit, he'd been drugged.

Turning, he saw a bivouac. He'd been lying on a groundsheet in front of the makeshift shelter, his head on a rucksack. He opened the pack.

Rope, a basic first-aid kit, Maglite flashlight, two-liter water bottle. Unscrewing the top, Dan drank deeply. Windproof lighter, water purification tablets. Sheath knife, Mars bars.

No map, no compass…no fricking indication of where he was. At the bottom of the rucksack was a tight bundle of clothing in a plastic bag. Dan unfurled it and stared. His black wedding suit, white shirt, taupe silk vest and matching tie.

There was an envelope in the breast pocket, under the taupe kerchief. He pulled it out and a yellow Post-it note fluttered to the ground. Ross had written *I will act like a girl.*

"Holy shit, I'm in the Ureweras."

Years earlier, on a training cycle his team had been dropped in this rugged national park with three days to reach a designated checkpoint while remaining undetected by a pursuit team. The Whakatane river had proved the most troublesome part of the exercise and Lee had related the legend of the Maori maiden.

In the absence of the men, Wairaka had retrieved a *waka*—canoe—which had drifted out to sea, shouting *Ka Whakatane au i ahau* as she paddled it back to land. I will act like a man.

In the miserable three days of training exercise that followed, it had become the team's catch-cry with one important modification. "I will act like a girl."

He tore open the envelope.

Dear Dan,
I can't undo the mistake of keeping you out of my treatment. I can only show you what faith I have in you for our future.

So, I'm falling backward, with my eyes closed and trusting you to catch me.

See you at the wedding.

xxx Jo

P.S. I know you chose ivory for the waistcoat and tie. But Barry talked me into taupe.

As he stared at the message, dumbfounded and appalled, drops of rain splattered on the page and blurred the kisses. *I'm marrying a scary, crazy woman.*

Carefully Dan dabbed the paper dry against his jeans, and slid it into his pocket.

Scary because he couldn't hide anything from her. Crazy because there was no way in hell he'd make it back in....

Pushing back his sleeve to check the time, Dan cursed. As a tracker, he'd been drawn to a watch with gadgets—GPS, distance timer. Ross had replaced it with his analog diver's watch. Knowing Ross, that meant Dan would be immersed in water somewhere on his journey. Grimly, he repacked his rucksack, rolling the contents in the plastic groundsheet first.

He had no idea where he was in those 213,000 hectares. He had no map but the hazy one in his memory, no compass, no communications. And when he got out of the park, nothing but his ability to persuade people to help him. Even once he reached a road, he was looking at a three-and-a-half-hour drive to Beacon Bay.

And the wedding was—he checked Ross's watch—in nine hours. Which left him five and a half to get out of here. "Jo," he groaned aloud. "What have you done?"

If the sun were shining he could have found north using the hands of the watch. Except there wasn't any sun. Mist hung over the forest like a shroud, diffusing the early morning light into an amorphous nothing.

Rain feathered through the mist, chilly and persistent on the back of his neck as he shouldered his backpack and walked into the forest, examining the foliage.

Dan quieted his mind, narrowed his focus and tried to recall everything he knew about the topography. The terrain was a series of fault lines, river-carved valleys and steep mountain ridges, thickly mantled by vegetation. The rivers flowed north.

Right now, he stood on the downward-sloping side of a small clearing. The chopper would have landed on a ridgeline. Most of the trees below were beech, a dominant species in the southern end of the ranges, which meant that civilization lay to the southeast.

In the Southern Hemisphere, the thickest

growth was to the north. Finding a broken tree, he checked the stump. The growth rings spaced more widely on the northern side.

Now he had orientation.

His best chance was in finding a river. Rivers were highways. There'd be trails, huts and people. But for now he'd skirt the ridgelines to avoid being boxed in. He didn't have time to retrace his steps. And being high would give him a vantage point when the mist cleared.

Before he left, he crossed some twigs in a marker, pointing the direction he would take. In case Jo came to her senses. Or Ross got cold feet.

Yeah, right.

"ARE YOU SURE YOU WANT to talk business now?" Grant shifted uneasily in his chair. "You're getting married this afternoon... wouldn't you prefer to concentrate on bridal stuff?"

Jo, Grant and Chris sat at a corner table in Shaker's. Around them the place was being transformed for her early-evening wedding reception. One person tied black bows around white-swathed chairs, another positioned wrought-iron candelabra holding silver tapers on white runners over black tablecloths, while a third buffed wineglasses.

Jo had chosen this day, time and venue precisely because she wanted to make Grant nervous. Chris frowned at his colleague. "She wants to tie up loose ends before she enters the next phase of her life, don't you, Jo?"

"Exactly," she said. *Assuming that door's still open.* "And since I've postponed this meeting twice already…"

Chris smiled. "Well, that sounds promising." He pulled a contract from his briefcase and pushed it across the starched tablecloth. "We made all the changes you requested…sponsorship, staff guarantees, et cetera."

She'd been playing with him, setting up a few hoops, throwing in a couple of loops. Accepting the paperwork, Jo pretended to read it.

There was another, private, reason for doing this now. She needed the distraction. Somewhere in the Ureweras, Dan was struggling to get home. What had he made of her letter? Had he understood any part of why she'd done this? Jo talked herself down. It was done now; all she could do was wait…and pray.

"Jo, you need a pen?" Chris proffered a black-and-gold Mont Blanc.

"Very nice," she said, turning it over to admire it.

"Keep it," he said magnanimously. "A goodwill gesture…no strings. Here, let me take the top off for you."

"Thanks." Jo handed him the pen. "So I have one question before we go any further." And though she knew that whether this worked or not she wouldn't be signing, her throat went dry. *What if I'm wrong and they're not bluffing? What if I've put the* Chronicle's *future… my staff's jobs at risk?*

Chris leaned forward. "Shoot."

"Excuse me, sir, may I put this on the table?"

Impatiently, he sat back and the florist positioned a glossy white box. Eight long-stemmed white roses sat on a bed of dark green ivy. Jo touched the velvety buds. "So Dan went for white, then."

The florist smiled at her. She looked like a flower herself with a vibrant, flowing top patterned in water lilies. "He liked the idea that white holds the potential to move to any color," she said, her long earrings tinkling as she gesticulated. "Psychically, it represents wholeness. New directions." She glanced at Chris, who was rolling his eyes. "It's so nice to meet a man with an open mind," she told Jo.

God, I hope so. She returned that sweet smile. "Thank you, you've done a wonderful job."

In a strange way it was calming to sit in the middle of this organized chaos—every perfectly executed detail a reminder of Dan's commitment. Please God, let him see her action in the same light.

"Jo," Chris prompted, placing the pen in front of her. "You have a question?"

She lifted her eyes from the roses. "Does CommLink really have plans to set up in opposition if I don't sell?"

"We've already established that," Chris said, then caught the direction of her gaze. "There's no point looking at Grant. He's not going to tell you any different."

"No, of course not…that would be unethical and Grant suffers from a conscience." Picking up the contract, she handed it back to Chris. "You know what? I'm going to take my chances. Grant, I don't pay nearly as well but you'll be able to sleep at night."

"You're trying to poach my staff in front of me?"

"Chris, you know I'd never say anything behind your back that I wouldn't say in front of you. You're an asshole. You used someone I grew up with as a stooge and you treated me like a patsy."

She stood to leave. "Oops, nearly forgot." She pocketed the Mount Blanc pen. "Thanks for the goodwill gesture."

The old gang had played a lot of poker in

their teens and Grant could never understand
why he was so bad at it. They hadn't told him
that whenever he tried a bluff on bad cards his
left eyelid would start to twitch.

DAN WAS TRAVERSING A BANK of scoria when it
began to shift. A few loose pebbles at first, skipping down the slope and disappearing sound-
lessly into the treeline. Others followed in a
loose, lazy slide, catching at his feet, sinking
him ankle-deep. Turning sideways to the slope,
he kept moving, fighting to stay upright.

The scree kept coming. He disappeared up
to his knees, hauling each leg out—desperate
now—eyes fixed on the edge of the forest. The
rumble grew to a roar. Glancing up he saw a
wave of bouncing rocks and pebbles tumbling
toward him and dived sideways, rolling the last
few feet into the shelter of the trees.

A small rock ricocheted off his left cheek,
leaving a sharp stinging sensation, a larger one
cracked him on the head. Dazed, he scrambled
the last few feet on hands and knees, coughing
as the dust cloud tickled his lungs and made his
eyes water.

He'd been a bloody idiot taking the risk, letting the time pressure get to him. The forest
sank back into silence. For a moment he lay in
the bracken, then Dan turned onto the backpack

with a groan, gingerly stretched out his limbs
and tested his joints. He was okay. Covered head
to toe in dust, but okay.

*When I said act like a girl I didn't mean a
dumb blonde,* Lee said and Dan laughed shakily. Great. Now he was hallucinating voices.
Pushing to his feet, he drank from the water
bottle and ate a Mars bar.

The clouds were clearing, enough to get a
reading on the sun. But mist still obscured the
lower reaches, which meant he couldn't risk
going down and getting lost. Aiming the hour
hand in the sun's direction, he bisected the angle
between the hour hand and twelve to find a
rough north.

Trying not to notice it was nine-fifteen.

Thirty minutes later the weather had closed
in again. Dan swore as he alternated left and
right around obstacles to counter a tendency to
veer in one direction.

Having to constantly look forward and back
to line up the two landmarks that kept him in a
straight line had seriously slowed his progress.
And he still had no idea how much farther he
needed to go.

Mentally, he adjusted his calculations. Three
and a half hours' drive could be reduced to three
if he drove like a bat out of hell. Assuming he
could beg a car. And Jo would wait.

Shit. He turned to check his landmark, found it obscured by a swirl of mist and stopped waiting for it to clear. Shit, shit, shit. At least his forward mark was still visible—just.

A rusa stag appeared in the dense scrub below him and Dan froze. This one was a beauty, deep red with antlers growing up three by three—six points. A wily animal to escape hunters for so many years.

The mist rolled around and between them like broken clouds. For all the movement, the air was quiet. The animal stopped grazing and raised its head, nostrils flaring and flanks heaving as it caught his scent. It looked straight at him with dark velvety eyes. Unaccountably his own filled with tears.

Last time he'd walked here, he'd been one of five young men, honing skills that would take them through a decade of soldiering together. A sob ripped through him and the stag vanished between one blink and the next.

Sinking to his knees on the rocky outcrop, alone with no witnesses, Dan laid his cheek against the cold stone and cried.

The wind gradually numbed the lobes of his ears under the woolen beanie. Finally lifting his face, he closed his eyes and imagined it blowing through him. Slowly, peace filled the hollow places inside him and Dan remembered not what he'd lost but what he'd been left. And who.

Sunlight hit his eyelids and he opened them. The cloud and mist were starting to evaporate. In the valley below the river winked in a shaft of sunlight and was gone. But he had a fix on it now.

Standing, he rubbed his wet eyes and his knuckles came away a dust-streaked gray. Wiping them dry on his jacket, he started down. While he jogged, Dan thought of Ross, scarred and driven by vengeance; Claire and Lewis, struggling to make sense of the senseless; and Nate, who'd cut himself off from the only family he had.

One of them had to take the first step on the road back. He had to win this one, not just for him and Jo but for all of them.

In the end, there was only one way to lead.

By example.

CHAPTER TWENTY

PAT STEPPED BACK WITH the makeup kit and Jo's face reappeared in her bedroom mirror. She blinked in surprise. "Well?" Pat prompted.

"Forget Dan," said Jo. "I can do better." Her eyes had been highlighted with a smoky gray shadow, lashes lengthened, skin tone taken back to flawless porcelain.

Pat laughed. "Too late now."

Jo smoothed out the skirt of her wedding gown and tried not to look at her watch, a delicate silver thread on her wrist, sparkling with marquisette. She'd only checked it a few minutes ago. It was twelve-thirty. And not a peep from Dan.

"Every bride suffers the jitters." Pat twisted one of Jo's red curls so it spiraled artfully over her left eyebrow, then smoothed the lace on the short sleeves. "You'll be fine."

"Of course I will." Standing, Jo took a spin in front of the mirror. "You made me beautiful," she said and hugged her future mother-in-law. "Thank you."

Pat fumbled for a tissue on the dressing table and dabbed carefully under her eyes. "Don't you dare make my mascara run."

There was a tap on the door and Ross's dark head appeared. "Ready?" His mouth was grim, which meant he hadn't heard from Dan either. Ignoring a flutter of panic, Jo picked up her beaded white bag.

"Ready."

"You might at least compliment the bride," Pat complained.

The best man cast a perfunctory scan over Jo's appearance. "Gorgeous." Silver eyes met hers, steely with anxiety. "Shall we go?"

Jo picked up the skirt of her gown and started downstairs, her dress a slither of cool silk against her legs. "Relax," she said to Ross. "There's still plenty of time."

"And it does make sense to visit Rosemary first." Pat had misinterpreted the comment. "But it is a shame Dan's seeing you before the ceremony. Is he downstairs, Ross? Let me look at him."

"He was running late," Ross lied smoothly, "so I said I'd pick Jo up first and then go back for him."

"That's not like Dan." In the hall, Pat gave Jo the soft white stole that would keep her warm en route to the church. "I thought you weren't supposed to be driving yet."

He wasn't. Jo answered for Ross. "Something came up last minute on the farm, I expect." Hold steady, she told herself, no wobbles. She draped the stole around her shoulders and gave her appearance a perfunctory check in the mirror.

"Nip that in the bud right now," warned Pat. "You don't want Dan ending up like Herman. So how are the nerves, Jo?"

She smiled. "I'm holding them at bay."

"By rights Jo should be a basket case," Pat commented to Ross. "Her bridesmaid is missing in action, Tilly tore a flounce on her flower girl's dress and Merry's had to rush her to the dressmaker's for emergency repairs. And what did Jo do this morning but go to work!"

"Deadlines," Jo said. "You learn to live with them."

Ross massaged the groove between his eyebrows. "Your bridesmaid's missing?"

"Not exactly." Patiently, Jo waited for Ross to open the front door. "Delwyn sent a text to say her future happiness was at stake, that she'd meet us at the church and she knew I'd understand."

Pat frowned. "You'd think it could have waited."

"I *do* understand," Jo said.

Ross closed his eyes briefly, as if for strength, and finally reached for the door handle. In passing, Jo patted his forearm. "You look handsome." He wore a suit like Dan's, charcoal black, except without a waistcoat. Jo straightened his taupe tie. "I think Barry was right about this color."

Outside the day was still overcast and a light wind chilled her exposed skin. She refused to shiver.

Ross had driven over in Dan's ute; from here they'd travel in the bridal car, a white Daimler polished and decorated with white ribbons that had been delivered earlier.

"I think I left a key in Dan's car," Jo said. "Won't be a moment."

Walking over to the ute, she opened the driver's door. As she'd hoped, Dan's Swanndri hung over the back of the seat. Making sure she wasn't seen, she leaned forward and pressed her nose into the wool, breathed deeply, then straightened, shut the door and returned to the Daimler. "Ready," she said, pretending to close her beaded bag.

"Let me grab my camera," Pat said. "Jo, you look a picture. Any man would be lucky to have you."

"Good," Ross muttered as they waited for Pat. "We might need a stand-in."

"That's the best man's job," she deadpanned.

He smiled suddenly, the harsh lines of his face relaxing. "You've heard from him. You wouldn't be this calm otherwise."

"No."

Pat came back and snapped a couple of shots. Jo settled in the back of the car, fanning out her white skirt.

"So rendezvous at the church in a few hours," Pat said.

Jo smiled. "See you there."

Ross eased into the driver's seat and started the engine. Waving a cursory farewell to Pat, he pulled out of the driveway, "Whatever you're taking, I want some."

"He'll be here," Jo said and shivered.

Ross said nothing, but he turned the heat on high.

"He'll be here," she repeated.

"I don't blame you," he said, "I blame myself. You don't know the Ureweras. I do. There's plenty of hazards to trip up a guy in a hurry…I didn't even leave him a goddamn compass."

"Don't start melting on me now, Icecream."

"I hadn't anticipated having to lie to his mother."

"A white lie. No point worrying anyone until…*unless* we have to. Now pull over and let me drive. I can see it's painful for you."

As usual he ignored her. "If we haven't heard from him by the time we get to the church I'm calling in a search party."

"When he's thirty minutes late," she said evenly, "you can start pushing alarm buttons. Until then you're doing what I'm doing."

"What's that?"

She noticed her hands had clenched in her lap. Jo uncurled her fingers, laid them flat and wide on the silk georgette. "You're believing in him, Ross."

DAN STOOD ON THE BANK studying the river. If water levels had been low he could have walked across; high he could have floated. Instead the river was neither one, which meant plenty of hazards lay hidden just under the surface.

Using his hunting knife, he finished trimming the twigs off the sapling he'd chosen as a walking stick and eyed it critically. Good enough. Then he stripped to his underwear, shivering as the cold wind goosed his skin.

With quick economy, Dan rolled his clothes tightly in the polypropylene groundsheet and jammed them inside the rucksack, then put his boots on over his bare feet. Slinging the pack over one shoulder so he could shrug it off if he got swept away, he waded into the river.

The water was so cold it made his toes ache

and by the time it swirled around his knees, his feet were numb. Using the stick as a probe, he shuffled across the riverbed at a forty-five-degree angle.

The water rose to mid thigh and lapped at the hem of his boxers, wicking up the silk until, wet, it clung to his ass. Ignoring the discomfort, Dan focused on finding footholds in the slippery, river stones. The toe of his boot jammed in a crevice. Bracing himself with the stick, he wiggled it free.

Two-thirds of the way across, the stick missed the bottom and disappeared under the fast-flowing water. Frustrated, he looked at the opposite bank, tantalizingly close, then downriver to where the channel narrowed and foamed between glistening rocks. If he had to swim, he needed a bigger margin of error.

The alarm on his watch beeped 12.30 p.m. Dan hesitated.

You won't be any good to Jo drowned.

"Son of a—" Shuffling his way back to the bank he'd just left he got dressed, frozen hands fumbling with zips and buttons, cursing himself warm. He wouldn't make it in time, had no fricking *hope* of making it in time. If Jo didn't know that, Ross did. He would kill his so-called wingman when he got back. Slowly, torturously, painfully.

Hell, he might as well slow down…viciously Dan reshouldered the pack…take his time, enjoy the goddamn walk.

He broke into a jog.

It took twenty minutes he didn't have anymore to find the right place to cross. Stripping again, Dan emptied his water bottle for extra buoyancy and packed it in the rucksack. Then holding it out in front of him, he launched into the water and started kicking.

Halfway across he spotted a telltale ribbon indent snaking across the muddy water ahead of him—an underwater snag. He flattened out, hoping to float over it but the strap of the pack caught, swinging him around and downstream. His grip on the canvas tightened. The strap held, water gushed around the pack as he bobbed in front of it like a human starfish.

A dozen thoughts raced through his mind.

My wedding suit is in there.

Like you have a hope in hell of making it now.

Let go.

Twisting his head with the flow of water he saw there was still a clear run to the bank. His biggest risk in holding on was hypothermia. Every two minutes his body was losing another one degree Celsius. Nine minutes and he'd pass out.

With monumental effort, Dan hauled himself closer to the pack and, ducking his head, fumbled under the surface trying to find where the broken sapling held the strap. Water poured up his nose. He lifted his head, gasping and coughing. One arm hugging the bobbing pack, he strained with numb fingers for the knife sheathed in the net side pocket, clamping his fingers around it through sheer force of will.

Gritting his chattering teeth, he sawed at the resistant strap. The pack shot toward him, slamming into his face and nose. Dan almost dropped the knife and grabbed it in a death-grip, rolling the rucksack downstream while he started kicking toward the opposite bank. His legs jerked feebly.

In a last frantic flounder he kicked to where the water eddied and slowed and grabbed a clump of trailing tussock grass. As he staggered onto the muddy bank his legs gave way and he toppled forward. For a moment he lay gasping, then hauled himself up to higher ground.

With violently shaking hands, he wrestled with the pack's straps and dragged out his dry clothes. It took him fifteen minutes to dress himself, piling everything on—the long johns, the wedding suit, the Swanndri and beanie.

Then, stumbling around like an old man, Dan gathered driftwood and made a fire, sitting as close as he dared, wrapped in the ground sheet. He choked down another couple of energy bars while he set river stones at the edge of the fire. When they were warm, he stuck them under his armpits and between his thighs, letting the major arteries there carry the heat around his frozen body.

It seemed hours before the tremors stopped and feeling returned to his extremities. Anxiously checking the time, Dan swore. The face had been cracked during his river swim and was full of water, the hands paralyzed at one o'clock.

He tried to think positively.

At least he was on the right side of the river.

Dousing the fire, he tied a knot in the backpack's broken strap, then reshouldered it and followed the current, his desperate gaze scanning the surrounding terrain. Within half a kilometer he spotted an old trail marker.

Finally, he had a route out.

"I HAD A DRESS LIKE that once." Nan leaned over the teacups to finger the material of Jo's skirt with her good hand.

"This is your wedding dress," Jo reminded her patiently. "You made it, right down to sewing all these Swarovski crystals on by hand. And when

Pops saw you in it, his eyes nearly popped out of his head."

"Pops?"

"Graham."

"Graham...yes," said Rosemary thoughtfully. "But should you be wearing it while we're planting? It might get dirty."

When Jo and Ross arrived, she'd been in the garden checking on her seedlings and had come inside for afternoon tea reluctantly. This wasn't the visit Jo had hoped for.

"Let me show you this special photo album I made you." Jo moved to sit next to her grandmother on the couch, picking up the album she'd dropped off earlier. She'd chosen the photographs carefully, leaving out any pictures that evoked sadness—Jo's mother, Pops as an old man shortly before he died.

She'd designed the album solely as a testament to her grandmother's many achievements—Rosemary hosting a *Chronicle* fundraiser, Rosemary behind the Thrift shop counter, Rosemary accepting a prize for her preserves, and, Jo's favorite, Rosemary encouraging Jo through the gate on her first day at school while Jo clung tightly to her grandmother's hand.

Jo reached for it again now, but Rosemary pulled it free to turn another page.

"I was quite something, wasn't I?"

"Yes, you were."

At least she didn't have to explain Dan's absence, except to the curious staff. Nan hadn't remembered she and Dan were visiting, let alone that her granddaughter was getting married within the hour. Polly was on stand-by to bring Nan to the wedding if Jo thought she was up to it, but clearly she wasn't. Besides, Jo couldn't be sure there'd *be* a wedding.

Or even that Dan would still want to marry her.

Stop it. Stop thinking like that. She couldn't afford to let doubt in now, even for a second. *We'll make it.*

Rosemary pushed the album aside and stood. "I need to get back to the garden now."

Jo had hoped for a much longer visit. Swallowing her disappointment, she also stood. "Absolutely, if that's what you want." So they wouldn't make a connection on her wedding day. She didn't have to make it this important. It didn't have to be an omen.

Ross entered the lounge. He'd been outside calling Father O'Malley in case Dan had already shown up at the church. Catching Jo's eye, he shook his head, then noticed she and Nan were standing. "Your visit's over already?"

"Nan's very busy in the garden today," she said cheerfully. "Nan, this is Ross." They'd already been introduced but he had been gone ten minutes.

Ross limped forward to shake her hand and Rosemary frowned. "You hurt your leg...you should rest it."

"That's what I keep telling him," said Jo.

"You should listen to Jocelyn," Unexpectedly Nan turned and gave her a sweet smile. "You're a good girl," she said. "A good girl, my darling."

Caught by surprise, Jo felt tears start to her eyes. She *couldn't* cry, Nan would get upset. Helplessly she looked at Ross.

"I've always wanted to grow vegetables," he said, drawing Rosemary's gaze. Jo had briefed him on suitable conversational openings. "But I don't know where to start."

Nan beamed. "Well, you've come the right person." She sat down again. "First, you need good compost, and I don't mean that rubbish they sell at garden centers. Jocelyn, come and tell...what's your name again?...Ross? Jocelyn, come and tell Ross what I've taught you about compost."

The Iceman poured tea and handed around lemon cakes while Jo extolled the virtues of humus and potash, seaweed and worm farms. Nan took her hand and squeezed it approvingly.

I can do this, Jo thought with strengthened resolve. *We can do this.*

"Of course," she said reflectively, "Ross already has a working knowledge of manure."

CHAPTER TWENTY-ONE

DAN LEANED HIS ARMS on the dash of the ancient Holden ute and hid his exhausted face against them. Through the damp Swanndri he smelled cracked vinyl and dust.

"You wanna call her, mate?" said his rescuer, Hone, an old Maori hunter who'd picked Dan up on the edge of the ranges. "Tell her you won't make it? I got a cell you can borrow."

"Yeah…thanks."

As Hone pulled over, Dan sat up and took another look at the time on the dashboard clock—2:05 p.m.—then dialed Jo's cell phone number. But somehow he couldn't bring himself to push Send.

Hone looked at him sympathetically. "You don't like disappointing your old lady, eh? But the only way you'll get there now is if you grow some wings and fly."

Dan stared at him. Then he dropped the cell, grabbed the old man's face between his hands and planted a smacking kiss on his tattooed forehead.

"Jeez, mate, you're back on the market quick."

"Can I make another call?"

"Sure."

Dan rang directory and got the number he needed. Then, heart in his mouth, he called Frank McBride. When he hung up, Hone was already driving toward Holyoake.

Taking off his watch, Dan dropped it into his new friend's lap. "I know it's broken but it's all I've got. And it will still net a hundred at least."

Hone tossed it back. "Nah, mate, happy to help. Besides, it's not yours to give away is it?"

"Ross won't need a watch where he's going."

Hone gave a wheezy chuckle, but still wouldn't accept it. "Come back and hunt with me sometime." He coaxed the shift stick into gear. "I didn't know Beacon Bay had an airfield."

"It doesn't." The closest lay across the bay in Totara. "Like you said, mate, I have to grow wings." Leaning forward, Dan scanned the sky. The weather was closing in again. He wasn't home yet.

He only realized he'd sworn when Hone stepped on the gas.

ROSS SNAPPED HIS CELL SHUT and turned from the steering wheel to look at Jo. "That was Pat. Very politely asking where the hell we are."

They'd been parked a couple of miles from the church for thirty minutes, delaying their arrival. After all, Dan *was* supposed to be with them.

Jo looked out the window at the spire in the distance, heard the bells herald four o'clock—the scheduled start of her wedding.

"What do you want to do?"

She sighed, then straightened her shoulders. "I guess it's time for an explanation." Ross started the engine while she packed up the playing cards. "And you owe me twenty bucks," she added.

Jo hoped that was simply because he was a bad card player and not because he knew the dangers facing Dan.

"Consider it my fee for aiding and abetting, Swannie," he said.

The church sat isolated on a small headland jutting into the sea, one of those picturesque early colonial buildings featured in tourism campaigns. White clapboard, steep pitched roof, arched, stained-glass windows. The gardens had been planted by early missionaries pining for home and comprised wind-twisted magnolias and camellias and a lawn of crunchy kikuyu grass salt-frosted a permanent maize-yellow.

As they pulled up, Jo saw Herman and Pat hovering on the steps. Tilly, cute and sullen in her flower girl's dress, stood behind them. Herman had the door open almost before the vehicle stopped. "I told Pat you couldn't hurry your visit," he said, then frowned. "Where's Dan?"

Jo gave him her hand to help her out. "Why don't I tell everybody at the same time," she suggested. Gathering her skirt, she started up the steps.

"It's my fault," Ross confessed.

"What's your fault?" said Pat. "What's going on?"

"Dan's been delayed," Jo said calmly. Her gaze clashed with Ross's. "But he'll *be* here."

His jaw set. "If we haven't seen or heard from him in half an hour—"

"Okay." Jo continued up the stairs. She wouldn't panic yet.

A low hum of conjecture followed her down the aisle but by the time she'd reached the pulpit she could have heard a pin drop. Father O'Malley said anxiously, "Is everything all right, Jocelyn?"

"It's fine." She looked around the curious faces of her friends and community and smiled. "I want to thank you all for your patience and reassure you that the groom's on his way. I arranged to have him helicopter-dropped in the

Ureweras overnight so you'll understand his delay."

Out of the corner of her eye Jo saw Ross put a hand over his face.

Every adult in the congregation stared at her. Only the kids returned her smile. Unconcerned, Merry's one-year-old, Harry, chewed on a hymnbook.

Herman turned to Ross, bewildered. "Is this a joke?"

"No," said Ross. "Like I said, this was my fault."

"It was my idea," Jo interrupted. "He'll be here."

"So you've heard from him then?" the priest asked.

"No," she admitted, "but I don't think he'll phone unless he can't make it."

"But what if his cell's flat, or lost or out of range?" called Pat.

"That's impossible," said Jo, "since we didn't give him one. However, I'm sure he's resourceful enough to borrow one."

Another stunned silence.

Pat turned to her soon-to-be ex husband. "Aren't the Ureweras hours from here?"

Herman nodded. "I've been hunting there," he said slowly. "It's no walk in the park." Again he turned to Ross. "Was this some kind of stag-night trick?"

"Yes," said Ross.

"No," said Jo. "This was something private between Dan and me."

"Did you two fight?" Father O'Malley asked. "Is that what this is about?"

"No, but it's a great idea as a future punishment," she joked.

More stares. It was like being back in the paddock with those unblinking bulls. Jo managed a smile. "Anyway, feel free to talk among yourselves and stretch your legs while we're waiting." She stepped down from the pulpit. People started talking in low voices, sending her lots of sidelong glances. Pat approached with a steely glint in her eye. Herman started questioning Ross.

Jo's cell rang in her beaded white bag. Her fingers trembled as she fumbled with the delicate catch to pick up. "Hello?"

"Don't start without me, we're nearly there," Delwyn said breathlessly. "And, oh, Jo, I'm married! I went to Wayne and told him I wanted him, not the trappings. And he said prove it, so we went to the registry office with our license, only there was a queue and—"

"Delwyn," Jo interrupted. "Tell me when you get here, okay? I need to keep the line free."

Flipping the cell closed, she stood. "My brides-maid," she told the congregation. She caught Ross checking his watch. "I still have twenty-two minutes," she said defiantly.

But Delwyn's call had shattered her compo-sure, left Jo feeling like she was clinging to a cliff-face by her pearly painted fingernails. She took a fortifying breath.

But she was still clinging.

"LOW THICK CLOUD UP NORTH," pilot Frank McBride shouted over the Cessna's engine. "If visibility is as bad as I think it is…"

They'd have to land in Totara. Waiting at the flight door, Dan looked at his new borrowed watch—4:07 p.m.—then at Frank. Glancing over his shoulder, the older man grinned. "I'll circle a third time," he yelled.

Frank had set up a tandem parachuting and skydiving operation out of his hometown, Holyoake, on his retirement from the SAS, some twenty-odd years earlier.

Now in his early sixties, the former air trooper still wore his famous handlebar moustache, and the gentle spread of middle age had given him the semblance of a benign walrus.

Parachuting was a basic skill in the SAS but those in air troop took it to the highest level, able to jump at altitudes high enough to freeze

Frank's facial hair, as well as at elevations that even experienced skydivers would consider dangerously low.

Dan hailed from mobility troop, a ground force, and hadn't thrown himself out of a plane for eighteen months. Frank had stroked his moustache when he heard that, but as Dan pointed out, he wasn't looking to freefall. A simple static line would do.

What neither of them could control was the weather. The clouds parted only enough for glimpses of land, nothing to help Dan get a visual on the chosen drop zone, the school football field a kilometer from the church.

He was perfectly capable of landing on the rectory lawn but, given he and Frank were civilians now, and Frank had a commercial license to protect, they were sticking to the rules.

And the rules said a drop zone of 100 by 100 meters square, clear of trees, fences, buildings and telephone wires.

Frank's son, Tom, who was operating the flight door, tapped Dan on the shoulder. "You're cutting it fine, mate. Think you should phone her?"

Dan shook his head.

Maybe it was crazy, but he believed phoning would be breaking faith with her. Jo believed he'd make it and he believed she'd wait.

Another glance at his watch: still 4:09 p.m. But how long would she wait?

"Look!" Tom pointed over his shoulder. A break in the cloud revealed the slash of narrow football field like a green flag.

"Door!" Dan hollered. A blast of wind buffeted them as Tom acted. No time for thanks, already the cloud was closing. Hanging his feet outside the aircraft, Dan launched, stomach swooping in the brief plummet before his parachute deployed, jerking his body up and back. Legs swinging, he grasped the toggles on the end of the steering lines, using them to line up the field, then slow him down as it rushed toward him.

Two barefoot kids were kicking a rugby ball on the field as he sailed over the goal post. They stopped to stare, heads flung back, mouths gaping as he landed a few hundred yards in front of them.

As he pulled in the billowing fabric, they arrived panting. "That was so cool, mister," one of them said.

He unclipped the harness, bundled the chute. "You two live close by?"

"Behind the school." The taller one jerked his head at a house beyond the trees. He was about fourteen with a friendly, open face. "I'm Simon Craft and this is my brother, Billy."

"Can you do me a favor, Simon?"

"Sure."

"Will you take the chute and gear to your house? I'll send someone back for them soon."

"Heck, yeah."

Removing his helmet, Dan stripped off his jumpsuit to the tux underneath. The younger boy's eyes widened like saucers. "Are you James Bond?"

Dan looked down at his tux—crumpled and streaked with dried dirt and blood—and laughed. There had been no time to clean anything but his hands and face. And even that hadn't made much improvement. There was a graze across one cheekbone, a bruise on the bridge of his nose where the pack had hit him. And yet he felt…free. Alive and exhilarated.

"No, son, I'm a farmer and I'm late for my wedding. I'll come back and tell you about it later." He handed the bundle to the older boy. "Take good care of it."

Simon's skinny arms tightened around it. "I will."

It was 4:25 p.m. Dan broke into a run.

AT 4:29 P.M. JO'S HEART leaped as the church door banged open, the sound echoing around the interior. A few people stood in the pews stretching their legs, most still sat, but every head turned. Delwyn burst in, wearing her midnight-blue bridesmaid dress—apparently Dan had balked at slimming black—and hauling Wayne behind her.

"Sorry...sorry I'm so late. Have you been waiting forever?" Pushing Wayne into one of the pews she flew up the aisle, her shoes clattering on the wooden floor, and holding up her ring finger to Jo. After giving her an excited hug, she glanced around puzzled. "Where's the groom?"

Disappointment crushed the last of Jo's courage. Dropping her bag, she sank down on the altar step, her gown spreading around her. "Okay," she said to Ross. "Call for reinforcements."

The best man opened his cell, hesitated and then snapped it close. "Or we could give him ten more minutes?"

No way could she let Ross Coltrane win this game of chicken. Jo held out her hands and let him pull her to her feet. For a moment she tightened her grip. "Thanks."

"It's only because I don't want to be the stand-in." They smiled at each other.

Incredulous, Pat glanced from Ross to Jo. "This has gone far enough. Dan could be lying unconscious somewhere…hurt…bleeding. I won't allow it."

Herman put an arm around Jo's shoulder. "Ten more minutes," he said to Pat.

"No, this is ridiculous." Pat appealed to the congregation. "Who's on my side?"

Debate broke out, growing in volume as contrary opinions were aired. Jo nearly missed the ring of her cell phone. She dived for her bag. "Hello?"

"Why did you do it?" Dan asked.

Throat tight she turned her back on the congregation, which hushed as people realized she was on a call.

"I thought," she croaked, started again. "I thought you needed this." Her next words came in a rush. "Tell me you're okay. Please…you can dump me after that. I just need to know you're safe."

"I'm okay," he called from somewhere behind her. Spinning around, Jo saw him standing at the church entrance. She gulped as she took in his appearance.

"My suit," Barry said faintly, from the end of one pew.

Dan shrugged. "I told you taupe wasn't my color."

The single-breasted black jacket and trousers were rumpled and muddy, there was a rip on one knee and the shiny waistcoat and tie were stained with brown watermarks.

The white shirt had seen better days and the silk kerchief was a limp rag in the breast pocket. His hair was tangled, his jaw unshaven. A cut across the bridge of his nose was blooming into a bruise that suggested he'd have a black eye tomorrow.

He looked terrible.

He looked wonderful.

Under all the dirt and bruises Jo saw the kid who'd laughed when she'd punched him, who refused to be scared off from being her friend, her sidekick, her childhood rival. The soul mate who would shelter her when she needed refuge and spur her on when she faced challenges. A man as solid as a rock.

Out of the corner of her eye she saw Ross's shoulders slump in relief.

"You're back," she whispered.

Dan tossed the cell to the usher and grinned, his teeth very white against his tanned face. "You don't get rid of me that easy…I'd have been here earlier but I missed a jump across a ditch and twisted my ankle. I had to hobble the last half mile. So—" he raised an eyebrow "—we getting married or what?"

With a small cry, Jo flew down the aisle and hurled herself into his waiting arms, heedless of her dress. Only when she went to kiss him did he hold her away. "If you ever," he said sternly, *"ever* do anything as crazy as that again I'll—"

Jo closed the distance and pressed her mouth fervently to his. It was a kiss that tasted of river water and dust, a kiss that promised a future.

"Shep, what the hell took you so long?" Ross said when they finally broke apart. "Incidentally, I couldn't find Jo's ring anywhere. I hope you have it."

She laughed. He hadn't told her that. Maybe the Iceman had some cool in him after all.

Draping an arm around her, Dan shook his head. "You're fired, Coltrane. I need a best man I can trust. Lewis Davis, get up here."

In one of the front pews, Lewis stood up, shooting a nervous look at Ross, who winked at him. Lewis grinned. Beside him, Claire reached for a hanky.

"Obviously we can't get married now—not without a ring," Jo said provocatively.

Dan's eyes narrowed. "Oh, ye of little faith. Your ring's at the jewelers but I found this in the trash can outside. Thought it would be perfect, given our initial contract."

He reached in his pocket, then opened a dirty hand. A beer can tab glinted in the light streaming through the stained-glass window.

Jo inspected it. "Perfect," she agreed and turned toward the altar. Paused. "The chicken dance won't really be playing at our reception, will it?"

Dan grinned and offered his arm. "Let's get married so you can find out."

* * * * *

LARGER-PRINT BOOKS!
GET 2 FREE LARGER-PRINT NOVELS PLUS
2 FREE GIFTS!

Harlequin

Super Romance

Exciting, emotional, unexpected!

YES! Please send me 2 FREE LARGER-PRINT Harlequin® Superromance® novels and my 2 FREE gifts (gifts are worth about $10). After receiving them, if I don't wish to receive any more books, I can return the shipping statement marked "cancel." If I don't cancel, I will receive 6 brand-new novels every month and be billed just $5.44 per book in the U.S. or $5.99 per book in Canada. That's a saving of at least 13% off the cover price! It's quite a bargain! Shipping and handling is just 50¢ per book in the U.S. or 75¢ per book in Canada.* I understand that accepting the 2 free books and gifts places me under no obligation to buy anything. I can always return a shipment and cancel at any time. Even if I never buy another book, the two free books and gifts are mine to keep forever.

139/339 HDN FC69

Name	(PLEASE PRINT)

Address		Apt. #

City	State/Prov.	Zip/Postal Code

Signature (if under 18, a parent or guardian must sign)

Mail to the **Reader Service:**
IN U.S.A.: P.O. Box 1867, Buffalo, NY 14240-1867
IN CANADA: P.O. Box 609, Fort Erie, Ontario L2A 5X3

Not valid for current subscribers to Harlequin Superromance Larger-Print books.

**Are you a current subscriber to Harlequin Superromance books and want to receive the larger-print edition?
Call 1-800-873-8635 today or visit www.ReaderService.com.**

* Terms and prices subject to change without notice. Prices do not include applicable taxes. Sales tax applicable in N.Y. Canadian residents will be charged applicable taxes. Offer not valid in Quebec. This offer is limited to one order per household. All orders subject to credit approval. Credit or debit balances in a customer's account(s) may be offset by any other outstanding balance owed by or to the customer. Please allow 4 to 6 weeks for delivery. Offer available while quantities last.

Your Privacy—The Reader Service is committed to protecting your privacy. Our Privacy Policy is available online at www.ReaderService.com or upon request from the Reader Service.

We make a portion of our mailing list available to reputable third parties that offer products we believe may interest you. If you prefer that we not exchange your name with third parties, or if you wish to clarify or modify your communication preferences, please visit us at www.ReaderService.com/consumerchoice or write to us at Reader Service Preference Service, P.O. Box 9062, Buffalo, NY 14269. Include your complete name and address.

HSRLP11

The series you love are now available in

LARGER PRINT!

The books are complete and unabridged—
printed in a larger type size to make it
easier on your eyes.

♦ Harlequin® *Romance*

From the Heart, For the Heart

♦ Harlequin®
INTRIGUE
BREATHTAKING ROMANTIC SUSPENSE

♦ Harlequin® *Presents*~

Seduction and Passion Guaranteed!

♦ Harlequin® *Super Romance*

Exciting, emotional, unexpected!

Try **LARGER PRINT** today!

Visit: www.ReaderService.com
Call: 1-800-873-8635

♦ Harlequin®

A *Romance* FOR EVERY MOOD™